The Bushwhacker

A CIVIL WAR ADVENTURE

A Peachtree Junior Publication

Published by
PEACHTREE PUBLISHERS, LTD.
494 Armour Circle NE
Atlanta, Georgia 30324

www.peachtree-online.com

Cover and book design by Loraine M. Balcsik
Composition by Melanie M. McMahon

Manufactured in the United States of America

10 9 8 7 6 5 4 3 2

Library of Congress Cataloging-in-Publication Data

Garrity, Jennifer Johnson.
    The bushwhacker / Jennifer Johnson Garrity ; illustrated by Paul Bachem. –1st ed.
        p. cm.
    Summary: While the Civil War rages in Missouri and Rebels destroy their farm home and scatter their family, thirteen-year-old Jacob and his younger sister find refuge in an unlikely place.
    ISBN 1-56145-201-7
    1. Missouri—History—Civil War, 1861-1865 Juvenile fiction. [1. Missouri—History—Civil War, 1861-1865 Fiction. 2. United States—History—Civil War, 1861-1865 Fiction. 3. Frontier and pioneer life—Missouri Fiction.] I. Bachem, Paul, ill. II. Title.
    PZ7.G1855Bu 1999
    [Fic]—dc21   99-26029
                                                                        CIP

The Bushwhacker

A CIVIL WAR ADVENTURE

Jennifer Johnson Garrity

Illustrated by Paul Bachem

PEACHTREE

ATLANTA

In memory of my grandmother, Zorah Knight Johnson Pinasco
and
To Shirley Brown, who taught me to love books.

—JJG

"*He that imposes an oath makes it,*
Not he who for convenience takes it.
Then how can any man be said
To break an oath he never made?"

—Samuel Butler

Table of Contents

Acknowledgments

I would like to thank the librarians at the American Studies Center at the Royal Library in Brussels, Belgium, for their consistent and cheerful helpfulness. Thanks also to Ron Pen (Associate Professor and Director of the John Jacob Niles Center for American Music at the University of Kentucky) for providing me with the songs "Shady Grove" and "Brightest and Best." Special thanks to Professor Michael Fellman (Simon Fraser University, British Columbia) for historical advice.

Most of all I want to thank Kathleen Istudor for her invaluable help and encouragement, and Kim, Kelsey, Collin, and Eliza Garrity for their patience and love.

Introduction

Missouri was just about the worst place a person could live during the American Civil War. The slave state was Union by vote, yet many Missourians, including Governor Claiborne Jackson, sympathized with the Southern cause.

When Governor Jackson was chased out of Jefferson City by the Union army in the summer of 1861, many Missourians were outraged—even those who supported the Union. Federal troops from surrounding states poured into Missouri, taking control of the larger cities and railroads, often treating Missourians with unnecessary brutality.

Bands of civilian warriors, called bushwhackers, sprang up around the state. These pro-Southern guerrillas waged cruel war against the occupying Union troops as well as pro-Union civilians. Union sympathizers also formed their own guerrilla bands and terrorized Secessionists.

No one was safe. No one knew whom they could trust. Missouri's people, including my own great, great grandparents, lived in confusion and fear throughout the remainder of the war.

In no way do I wish to defend bushwhackers in this book. Neither do I defend the Union army's actions in Missouri. My desire is simply to tell Missouri's tragic and complex story.

—J. J. G.

October
Fire

OCTOBER, 1861

Missouri breathed slow and heavy that evening. Our corn hung dust-covered and still, and the fields were hushed except for the buzz of a few old crickets hanging on with the warm weather. I wiped sweat off my nose with the back of my hand, for my fingers were stained from squashing earworms I'd caught eating on the stalks. Pa'd said to leave them be, that the coming frost would take care of them good enough, but I didn't like to see anything or anybody tear down what we Knights had worked hard to build.

Muttering to myself, I wiped worm guts on my trousers. Where was Eliza? Why didn't she have to work extra like me at harvesttime? Well, I guessed I knew where she was. Sitting inside the house on her lazy hindquarters.

"Jacob, you go on picking in that back field till sundown," Pa'd said to me at the supper table. "Indian summer's almost used up, and winter's breathing hard down our necks."

Yes indeed, I carried my weight at corn-picking time, but Eliza flopped her skirts in the horsehair chair of an evening, doing her fancy needlework. It seemed to me that when I'd turned thirteen in spring, I was all of a sudden expected to do a man's share of the chores. Well, if it worked the same way with girls, I figured Eliza had it coming to her in about five years. She'd only just gone eight in June; old enough to do at least a child's share of the work, but I swear she didn't do even that much.

I'd just pinched another worm and flung it to the ground when our dogs started in yapping over by the house. A shout cut through the corn and stuck me sharp in the ear.

"Ezra Knight!"

Who wanted my pa that couldn't just come on up to the house and ask for him the way folk usually do?

"Ezra Knight!"

The hollering came from somewhere out front of the house. I stretched up on my bare toes and looked through the corn in that direction, but I couldn't see anybody. The sun was hanging low and the house lay west of the cornfield, so I didn't get much but an eyeful of sun.

I snapped off one last cob, dropping it in the leather-strapped basket slung over my shoulder. I'd been wishing the sun would sink down fast so I could quit. Now I had all the reason I needed. Digging a hole with my bare toes to mark my place in the row, I moved on down to the handcart sitting at the field's edge to dump my pickings. I was just pulling the basket strap over my head when I spied two horses circling our yard.

I stopped short, for the men who straddled them wore kerchiefs tied around their faces. My heart jumped up in my throat, sending blood pounding so loud in my ears the whole world went silent. Feeling my knees buckle, I dropped the basket and sank down behind the leafy stalks.

Being harvesttime, I'd been so busy corn picking that I'd left off worrying and fooled myself into thinking they'd never come.

But I ought to have known better. We were Union folk in a county full of Rebels; it was only a matter of time.

"Secesh!" I whispered, Secesh being what we called those Confederate Rebels wanting to secede from the Union. Anyone who didn't know all about the Rebel gangs we called bushwhackers would have been an ignorant soul indeed.

Bushwhackers had been strutting up and down our part of Missouri ever since General Price whipped the Yankees at Wilson's Creek in August. They got bolder and meaner with every barn they burned and every bridge they blew up. Running like wildfire all over the countryside, they took pleasure in tormenting good Union folk. Lately they'd been bragging that they were going to run every Union man out of Missouri by Christmastime.

Yes sir, bushwhackers were fierce, thieving murderers who fought for the South on their own terms, taking orders from no one. When I heard the older boys in Boonesboro whispering about them behind the livery stable, my hair stood on end. They said bushwhackers scalped their dead, just like Indians.

From my bed one night I'd heard Ma tell Pa how afraid she was. She asked him to cross us over the border into Iowa to live with her folks till the war ended, but Pa held fast.

"Missouri's a Union State by vote, Myra," he'd comforted her, "and the Union will protect its own."

The next day on the way out to the fields I'd asked him why Ma was afraid. He lay an arm across my shoulders and pulled me close to him. As we walked, he explained how things stood with Missouri.

"Jacob, ever since the country split in two last winter, you've known there are plenty of folks in this state who want to drag Missouri out of the Union, even though most want to keep her in."

I nodded. Of course I knew it.

"You've heard me say plenty of times that I'm a Union man, and you know that means I'm against secession. There's just no sense in splitting the country up, to my way of thinking. But most of our neighbors here in Howard county don't think that way."

"Why not, Pa?"

"Well, their feelings are all tied up with the Southern states—they're tired of the government over there in Washington telling them what to do. So they're hopping mad about Missouri going to the Union side, and it's getting harder and harder for folk like them to live peaceably with folk like us. There's a mess of anger on each side. Why, it's getting so a man can't even trust his neighbor."

"Will they try to hurt us, Pa?" I asked in a whisper.

He smiled. "Likely not, Jacob. That Secesh governor of ours got chased out of Jefferson City for good back in July. Missouri belongs to the Union now. Sure, that old peacock General Price is giving the Federals trouble, and Rebel bushwhackers are running wild all over the place. But more and more Yankee troops are slipping into the state. It'll likely take some time, but Federal troops will help keep those Secesh in their place. Like I told your ma, the Union will protect us."

As I crouched among the corn, keeping one eye on the back of the house, I hoped Pa's words were true. The sound of dishes rattling floated out the open back window along with little Sarah's chatter. I listened hard for the squeak of the front door and my pa's footsteps on the porch, but that sound didn't come.

Pointing rifles to the sky, the two masked riders paced back and forth, weaving their horses across the yard, trampling down Ma's garden. Where there were two I knew there'd be at least ten hiding in the woods nearby, for bushwhackers ran in packs, like slinking wolves.

The riders turned to black shadows against the blood-red sky, and I guessed they'd put themselves there on purpose to blind my pa as he looked out the window. Shielding my eyes, I squinted against the glare of the falling sun. I couldn't see the front of the house, but when Pa finally answered I could tell he stood at an upstairs window, probably with a rifle at the ready.

"What's your business here?"

"Ezra Knight!" called up one of the riders. "We got business with all the Lincoln-lovin' scum in Howard County. Come on down and answer for yerself!"

"You'd best move off my property!" shouted Pa. "I won't answer to you, nor anybody!"

A horse whinnied; the air hung silent except for the chirping of the crickets in the fields. Rocking on my knees, I squeezed my eyes shut tight. "Oh God, oh God, please, please, please!" I begged. "Make them go away!"

"We ain't gonna stand for Union trash in this county! It's you, Knight, that'll have to git off the property!" one of the men shouted.

"It's my farm and I'll stay right here!" yelled Pa. "A man's got a right to his own politics."

The two strangers snorted out a laugh before one of them answered, "Not in Missouri!"

The front door banged open. Ma's shrill voice burst out, "Leave us in peace, for God's sake!"

Little Jerusha cried out then. Her fretful howl turned something loose inside me. My family was in danger. What kind of shameful coward was Jacob Knight, cringing in a cornfield? No. I'd stand with Pa.

Springing to my feet, I tore across the yard, taking all three front steps in one leap. Ma stood on the porch with Jerusha in her arms and Sarah clinging to her skirts. Eliza cowered behind her in the doorway, her face white as a muslin bedsheet beneath her yellow hair. I spun around. The shadow-riders paced back and forth against the red glare of the sun.

"You hidin' behind yer wife's skirts, Ezra?" snickered one of the men, and the other roared out an ear-splitting guffaw. "This skinny boy of yers has got more gumption than you! It's you we want, not yer wife and kids!"

My face went hot and I felt my lips quiver with shame. How dare they insult my pa!

"I'll not come!" thundered Pa's voice from above, just seconds before a shot rang out. Ma's scream pierced the still air beside me and the whole world set to spinning.

Shot followed shot as I pushed Ma in the front door, with Jerusha, Sarah, and Eliza. I kicked it shut and bolted it. We huddled in a heap on the floor while Pa fired down at the bushwhackers and they fired up at him. A bullet shattered an upstairs window, raining glass down like hail on the porch roof. Another tore through the glass above our heads and nipped our mantel clock. Still another sent Ma's china bulldog flying across the room in a thousand pieces. Sarah burst into tears.

"Hush up!" I screamed. Ma reached out and pulled her close, whispering something in her ear as they lay side by side, surrounded by splintered glass.

Between shots I heard our dogs yapping in the fields and the chickens squawking. I buried my face in my hands, digging my fingernails hard into my scalp. "Oh God, make them go!" I prayed it hard, over and over, till smoke began to drift in through the broken windowpane, stinging my nose and eyes.

"Oh Lord, they mean to burn us out!" cried Ma, cradling Jerusha in one arm and pulling Sarah closer with the other. Eliza began to sob, burying her face in Ma's lap.

I raised myself onto my knees and looked outside. Sure enough, a dozen horsemen stampeded through our yard, waving lit torches above their heads and making straight for the barn. Full to bursting with summer hay, it quickly shot up in flames the color of the sinking sun.

Now the Rebel gang circled our house, whooping and hollering and swinging their torches.

"Jacob, get down!" hissed Ma, but I couldn't move. Feeling the horses' pounding hooves deep in my gut, my eyes locked on a rider making straight toward me. He turned his horse in the nick of time and streaked across the window, then circled around and trotted up close. He was so near I could smell the kerosene-soaked rag tied to the flaming stick he held. I could see the brown and white swirls on the horn-handled knife hanging from his belt. With one filthy paw he shielded his eyes and bent down to the jagged hole in the glass.

"Jacob!" Ma screamed, but I stayed put.

The bushwhacker shot his eyes around the room. As soon as they lit on me they opened wide, then wrinkled up at the corners as he gave a low laugh. His heaving breath sucked and puffed the kerchief in and out a few times before he growled, "Yankee trash!" Then he swung his torch above his head twice and sent it crashing through the remaining glass. The flying shards sent me wheeling backward, covering my face with my arms as the fiery missile flew over my head and landed on the rag rug near the hearth.

"The quilt!" shouted Ma.

I jumped up and made straight for Pa's rocker, grabbing the

quilt hanging on it and beating out the flames. But no sooner had I put the fire out than in shot another burning stick. I beat that fire out too, but more torches kept coming. Ma pulled herself up off the floor and dragged the three girls back into the kitchen.

"Jacob!" She flung the back door open. "Take Eliza. Run!"

I stood for what seemed like forever, staring at her face, at her wet cheeks shining in the eerie light of the barn fire. What could she mean, telling me to run off? Surely if we ran we ought to all run together! But she grabbed my shoulder and shoved me hard out the open door.

"Don't stand there like a fool. Run, boy!"

"But...but Pa—" I stammered.

"Run!"

So I ran, with Eliza right behind me.

Our horses were loose and the Rebels were tearing around, trying to catch them. Out of the corner of my eye I saw one leading our cow across the side yard toward the woods, and still another dragging a bushel of squash out of the burning barn. Our dogs yapped and howled; hogs ran wild in every direction, squealing and snorting and all but drowning out the shouting and gunfire. Between the almighty roar of the fire and the confusion in the yard, no one seemed to notice Eliza and me running toward the back fields. If they did, they didn't much care; they were too busy laying their thieving hands on all our goods.

We stumbled through the corn, the leaf blades cutting our faces, our bare feet tangling up in the stalks. Halfway through the field I heard Pa crying out in pain, sounding like a wounded animal.

"Pa!" I screamed, making to bolt back toward the house, but Eliza butted right into me and knocked me flat.

"No, Jacob! Ma said run!" Her pale blue eyes flashed in the fire's light.

"Pa's hurt!" I cried, pulling myself up by a broken cornstalk.

Eliza yanked me up by the arm and pushed me ahead of her. "You run, Jacob, like Ma said."

I wavered, caught between running on and turning back. Tears stung my eyes as I realized Eliza was right. Ma said to run. Surely she knew what she was doing. And I couldn't help Pa now. I turned and fled, pulling Eliza by the hand.

We ran till we'd cleared the plum thicket that backed up against the Fayette road, then we struck out northeast along it, Eliza clawing my hand so tight her nails dug into my skin. I dragged her along as fast as I could, for by now the sun was half gone, and darkness gathered around us. We ran till we sucked for air, but I kept moving though my bare feet throbbed with every step. By and by Eliza began to drag back, yanking on my shirtsleeve and whimpering.

"Jacob, wait—"

"Stop yankin' on me!" I jerked my arm away and wheeled around, all set to hush her, but I thought better of it when I saw her face, streaked with dirt and shiny with sweat and tears. She'd done all she could. She was only eight years old, after all.

When I'd caught my breath I took her hand and pulled her into a clump of bur oaks that grew between the road and the stream we called the Little Turkey. We lay down side by side in the brush, our breath coming hard. My whole body trembled, though I kept as still as I could. I put my arm across my sister, and felt her shaking too.

"We'll wait here," I whispered.

We lay quiet a long time, listening to the blue jays above us in the oaks. They rustled and flapped and moved through the treetops like they didn't know whether to roost or fly. "Thief! Thief!" they shrieked, like they'd seen what happened and meant to warn the whole countryside.

Wheels creaked by on the road, but not knowing who they belonged to, we stayed put, careful not to make a sound.

"Ma'll come and get us soon," whispered Eliza. "Won't she?"

"That's right."

She lay awhile without speaking. "And Pa," she added.

I could feel my eyes closing though I tried my best to keep them open. "Yes, and Pa," I murmured.

~

Just before dawn I woke up shivering, angry at myself for sleeping so long, knowing I ought to have kept watch. What if Ma and Pa had come along the road in the night looking for us, too afraid of the bushwhackers to call our names out loud?

I sat up in the grass and listened. The jays were calling sunup. Through the bur oaks I could see pink and orange streaks of light just above the horizon. The leaves stirred above me and a rooster crowed far off. A light, smoke-smelling wind rustled through the creek woods, and I hugged my knees under my chin to keep warm. Dragging my feet up like that nearly set me to howling, and for the first time I knew I'd run clean across broken glass putting out the fires.

While my fingers set to picking out the sharp glass splinters, my brain spun around and around. I knew Ma had stayed in the burning house so as not to leave Pa, and that Jerusha and Sarah were too little to run away with Eliza and me. Where were they now? I hung my head between my knees and hid in shame. I ought to have gone back for the little ones! I ought to have stayed and fought at Pa's side. But Ma had ordered me to run.

Our farm was a good eight miles from Boonesboro, the nearest town; we couldn't have reached there in time to send help. And as far as we could tell, all the folk on neighboring farms were Secesh. Ma could only have meant for us to lie low in the woods till the Rebels cleared out. Well, we'd done that. There was no use in us hiding any longer. It was time to head back home.

Reaching down, I shook Eliza awake. "Get up. We're goin' home."

She always was a quick riser. She got right to her feet, rubbing her eyes, then said she needed to go off and do some private business in the woods first.

I nodded. "Go on. But hurry. Ma and Pa'll be wondering where we are. And give me that white skirt you wear under your dress."

"What for?"

"Never mind. Just give it. Hurry."

She pulled it off and tossed it to me before going behind some trees. It took me the whole time she was gone to bite a hole in it with my teeth and rip it into strips.

"Jacob! What are you doin' with...Jacob, you're bleedin'!" she cried, kneeling down and staring at my feet, open-mouthed. "Oh, Jacob, you're hurt bad!" She began to whimper.

"Hush now, it ain't nothin'," I lied. "Just help me."

"Don't make me touch it!"

"I've picked out the glass!" I snapped. "Hand me the strips, that's all!" I wrapped my feet and tied the strips in knots at the top. When I'd finished, Eliza pulled me up and I limped as best I could toward the road, leaning on her shoulder.

Hobbling along the Fayette road, my hopes grew tall. I had faith in my pa. He was as good a marksman as I'd ever seen, one of the best in Howard County. I just knew he'd shot at least half those bushwhackers right off their saddles! Yes sir, my pa had likely sent those Secesh cowards hightailing it for the woods, running for cover clear into the next county.

"Jacob," Eliza interrupted my thoughts. "Our barn's burnt up. Do you think our house—"

"Naw!" I fairly shouted. "Now, Eliza, you saw me beat out those little fires. Ma could've done the same, after we left."

She sniffled. "But...but why didn't Pa come down and help us? Why didn't he take us all away from there?"

I stopped and turned toward her, my temper flashing hot and red. "Don't you say one word about Pa!" I snapped, grabbing her by the shoulders and giving her a hard shake. "They'd have killed him for sure, like they've been killin' Union men all over Missouri!"

Eliza choked on a sob and sniffed hard. "I didn't mean nothin' by it, Jacob. I was just wonderin'."

"Well, stop." I let her go and started on again.

We reached the plum thicket at the edge of our back field just as the bottom edge of the sun cleared the earth, then we picked our way through the undergrowth. When we cleared the thicket, Eliza made as if to bolt straight home. Yanking her back hard, I motioned for her to keep quiet. Smoke hung thicker here, and a heavy quiet lay over the fields. She looked up at me with her eyes wide and nodded her head. I let go again.

Dropping on all fours, I crawled out to the corn, waving for Eliza to follow. We crept low to the ground until I reached a spot where I thought I could best see the house. I stood up and pushed the leaves aside. What I saw stung like a dry hickory branch snapping into my face. A black, smoking shell stood where our house had been. Pieces of ash shot up from it with every little gust of wind, scattering across the fields. The barn that'd been near to twice as big as the house was nothing but a heap of charcoal.

Fightin' Tom, our rooster, strutted circles around the yard, crowing with all his might. All ragged and soot-covered, he jerked his head from side to side, looking around for his lady friends. Most likely they were all in Rebel stew pots by now.

"Pa!" I called, pushing through the corn. "Pa!" My voice cracked and floated up into the early morning sky along with some guilty crows. Eliza crept up behind me and slipped her hand in mine. I squeezed it tight.

"They're dead, ain't they, Jacob?"

"No! Don't say that. Ma! Ma, you come on out now! It's all right, those bushwhackers ain't here no more!"

The wind shook the corn and blew ash into our faces. Eliza choked and coughed, then started in sobbing. "Sarah!" she screamed above the rustling corn leaves. "Sarah, you stop hidin' from us!"

With eyes stinging from smoke and tears, we picked our way around the edges of the blackened ruin. We found charred pots and Pa's upturned rocker, still glowing red in places when a breeze touched it. At the sight of it, Eliza began calling out for Ma and Pa. But by the time the sun was high and had gone from orange to yellow, I knew they weren't coming.

"You sit here," I told her, pushing her down onto the ground. Choking on a smoky gust of wind, I fought hard against the one thought that just wouldn't clear out of my mind: only the worst would keep my folks from coming for Eliza and me. Could it be my family didn't escape those flames? Had Pa fought to the very end, and Ma stayed right there in the house with him? Then I searched a ways until I found me a good long stick. My stomach went sick as I walked toward the smoking ash pile, knowing what I had to do. Not two steps away from it, I stopped.

"No!" I screamed, whirling away from the ashes and heaving the stick deep into the corn. No. If that were so, Eliza and I were lost for sure. My hope was still alive, and I couldn't bring myself to kill it. A sudden thought struck me. I stepped toward my sister, glancing around the yard. "Eliza! Do you see the wagon anywhere?"

She got to her feet and looked around, shielding her eyes from the bright morning sun. "No, Jacob. You reckon those bushwhackers made off with it?"

"Could be," I answered. "But you remember the McRae family, don't you? How they got burned out near to two months ago? Bushwhackers set fire to their house, then cleared out. Well, they piled up their wagon with all they could save, then took off south, down Jefferson City way. I'll just bet Ma and Pa done the same thing!"

Eliza looked up at me with her muddy, tear-streaked face, her lower lip trembling. "Gone to Jefferson City? Without us?"

"Either that or Iowa," I said, remembering how Ma'd begged to go there. Ma's sister Lucille lived on a farm somewhere near Iowa City, but that was all I knew. I couldn't even recall her last name. I forced a smile. "Ma and Pa know we can catch up. Shoot, Eliza, we can do that easy."

"Well, which way, then, Jacob?" Eliza whined, as if I could know for sure.

"Just hush a minute, and let me think!"

Pa would surely move north, to Iowa, I decided. To push deeper into this God-abandoned state made no sense. Missouri had burst into flame and fallen to ash just as surely as our house and barn had done, and we had no more life here.

Union folk were sorely outnumbered in these parts, and I'd heard Pa say more than once that bushwhackers took off their masks by day, pretending to be law-abiding citizens. Who was to say the man who'd hurled a torch through our window wasn't someone we sold grain to in town, or even our nearest neighbor?

It was no easy thing to tell if a body were Union or Secesh these days, if that person wanted to keep it a secret. Just because a man owned a slave or two didn't mean he was Secesh. And not all Union families were like us; some kept slaves. No, Yankees and Rebels grew side by side in Missouri's garden; it was getting impossible to tell one from the other anymore. And if Pa didn't trust folk, neither did I. I wouldn't go looking for my family at a neighboring farm.

My throat squeezed up tight, nearly cutting off my breath, and my lips tingled cold with fury. "Burn in hell!" I screamed at all the Rebels in Missouri. A flock of crows lit out of the corn, squawking and beating the air like a hundred drums.

Fightin' Tom clucked and fussed and circled the yard, flapping ash-clouds off his wings. Eliza put a hand on my shoulder and gave it a shake. "How'll we find 'em, Jacob?"

I knew then that I was Ma and Pa to Eliza now. I bent my head and rubbed my forehead hard with a sooty hand. When I finally answered her, I tried to make my voice as steady and sure as I could, for her sake.

"We'll walk to Boonesboro. If we don't find 'em there...we'll head north, toward Iowa. Could be we'll catch 'em on the road." My eyes wandered over to Ma's trampled down kitchen garden. "Come on, Eliza, and help me dig!"

With our bare hands we dug up what carrots, turnips, and potatoes we could find, then picked off a little, green, late-planted pumpkin. Eliza made a sack with her apron, and I threw into it all that would fit, till it bulged out tight and almost ripped. Skirting the cornfield, we found only a pile of fresh-picked ears where the handcart had stood.

"I guess those thievin' maggots took more than they could carry," I said, stuffing as many of the ears as I could into my pockets. Then we pushed through the plum thicket toward the Fayette road.

I plunged headlong into the thicket on my torn-up feet, biting back the pain, eager to put miles between me and that ghost of a farm. We'd pushed near to halfway through when a sharp cracking noise sounded ahead of me. I backed up into Eliza; she dropped most of the vegetables and shrieked in my ear. A horse's whinny sounded ahead in the shady thicket. Twigs snapped and cracked as the horse moved toward us. Slapping my hand over Eliza's mouth, I pulled her back behind a plum tree.

Then I saw that it was Sally, the bald-faced mare Pa favored riding, still haltered up and getting caught on the branches because of it. She twisted her head from side to side, snapping twigs to get the halter free.

"So those greedy bushwhackers didn't make off with you after all!" I all but shouted, never so glad to see a horse in all my life. I let go of Eliza. Reaching up and stroking Sally's neck, I caught her by the throatlatch. She snorted, puffing her hot breath into my hand, then pushed her muzzle onto my chest, looking for something to eat. I reached down for a fallen carrot and fed it to her.

"It's all right, Sally," I whispered as she chomped it down. "I'm here. Thank God you're here too." I pressed my face into her cheek, grateful not to have to walk all the way to Iowa on bleeding feet.

It took some time to get Sally turned around and out onto the road, but we managed. Pa had trained her well; even bareback she was a good mount. When we'd gathered up the vegetables again and tied them up good in the apron, I climbed onto Sally's back, then pulled Eliza up. We set the apron sack between us, Eliza holding it tight with one hand and holding on to me with the other.

At first Sally made as if to run off in the direction of home. Without reins, it was all I could do to turn her around by yanking hard on her halter's left cheek strap. We turned circles three or four times in the road before I got it through her head we weren't going home. When she finally swung around to the south I kicked my bloody heels into her flanks, and we took off down the Fayette road toward Boonesboro.

The Road North

Noontime found us making one slow, weary ride up Boonesboro's main street. We must have looked a sight, all dirty-faced and loaded down with vegetables. Some folk watched us and some looked away as we passed, but whichever one they did I felt the same message coming through: This was a Secesh town and we weren't welcome here.

When we reached the square I watered Sally at the public well. Eliza sat down on a patch of grass, holding her apron sack in her lap. Shops were closing up for the noon hour; people hurried every which way across the square to get home for dinner. I did my best to catch each one by the eye as they passed us, trying to ask a silent question: What do you know about the goings-on at our farm last night?

I knew many of the Boonesboro folk by sight, our family having done business in that town since we'd come out from Ohio nine years ago. Most of them recognized me too, but no one stopped. Fact is, they looked down while they passed by, like they'd just bought new shoes and couldn't get enough of gawking at them.

Only Old Silas, the free Negro who owned the livery stable, opened his eyes wide and stopped short when he saw me. "Jacob Knight, what done happened to you?"

"Bushwhacked!" I answered.

"Lord have mercy!" He swung his gray head right and left before taking a step closer and whispering, "Burned out?"

"Yes sir, and I'm lookin' for my family. You seen 'em, Silas?"

He glanced around the square, then dropped his eyes to the ground and spoke as low as he could without whispering. "No, I ain't. And my guess is they ain't in this town. Shoot, I'm gettin' out of this town myself. Headin' for Kansas. Why'nt you head for Kansas too?"

"Naw," I said. "I guess our folks'll head north. We aim to catch up with 'em."

Silas gave a low whistle. "Have you gone crazy, boy? The whole countryside's full of Rebel ruffians! Besides, you got your little sister to think about now. How you gonna feed her?"

I pointed to the bundle of vegetables on Eliza's lap. Silas wrinkled up his eyebrows. "And the horse?"

"There's grass aplenty between here and Iowa," I told him.

"Grass! You expect that mare to carry you both that far, eatin' only grass? Boy, a load-bearin' horse needs grain. You know that!"

Of course I knew it. I'd just figured it couldn't be helped.

Silas glanced around the square. "Follow me down to the livery stable," he whispered. Then, whistling and nodding good day to folk who passed, he strolled on down the street with us behind him. When we reached the stable, he pulled open the big barn doors and led Sally inside. He lifted up each of her hooves to make sure she was well shod, which she was. Pa always took good care of his horses. Then he dipped into a barrel and filled two feed sacks with oats. "I ain't got much, but what I got, I'll give," he said. "At least that horse won't starve!"

Silas tied the top corner of one sack to the top of the other, then disappeared into the darkness at the back of the stable. We heard him rummaging around, whistling to himself. Then out he came with a saddle in his arms and a bridle slung over his shoulder.

"But Silas!" I objected. "I ain't comin' back this way again. I can't return it."

"Don't matter," he said, cinching the saddle strap around Sally's middle.

"You sure?"

"Boy, I told you I'm leavin' here for Kansas." He swept an arm around the stable. "I can't take all this with me!" He slipped the bridle over Sally's head, then led her to a feed box so she could get her fill before we set off. When she'd had enough, Silas helped Eliza and me into the saddle and slung the oat sacks over the horn. Then he took hold of Sally's lead and started for the door.

"The vegetables!" cried Eliza.

"Uh-oh. Don't want that horse eatin' better than you two." Silas picked up the apron sack and heaved it up to us. "Well, Jacob and Eliza, all I got to say is this: stay off the roads, 'cause horse thieves are sproutin' up thick as prairie grass since the war started. Now get yourselves out of here just as quick as you can, before Missouri swallows you up!" He slapped Sally's rump, and we burst out of the dark stable into bright daylight, galloping down the road so fast I could hardly thank him.

We made our way west to the Missouri River, aiming to follow it up to where the Grand splits off to the north. I knew Locust Creek ran straight down from Iowa and flowed into the Grand, because I'd followed it up as far as Laclede with Pa once, deer hunting.

We did like Silas said and stayed mostly off the roads. I knew he was right about the horse thieves. On account of the war, folk would pay a fancy price for a good mount, and even a flea-bitten nag could bring in near to twice what she was worth. Sally was a fine, strong mare and I didn't intend to lose her.

For three days we moved north, riding steady from sunup to noon. When the sun was high we'd wind our way down to the water's edge. There we'd eat our vegetables and water the horse before finding a thick growth of trees to hide in. In that shelter we'd stretch out and rest a few minutes before riding till sundown.

On the fourth day we reached the Locust. Sally carried us along beside the mud-brown water, keeping to a trail just above the river bottom. Once in a while we saw a farmer out corn-picking, or a slave boy driving cattle down to the water. I just nodded my head as we passed, and pressed on. No one asked us what our business was, and I was glad not to have to answer.

My insides stung like my glass-cut feet whenever I closed my eyes and saw my ma's face all twisted up with fear as she yelled at me to run. The sound of gunfire seemed to follow me along the quiet stream, echoing all around us in the silent trees. I stuck my fingers in my ears and shook my head hard, trying to fling it off, but it wouldn't go away.

Maybe I ought to have waited around Boonesboro till I figured out who'd bushwhacked us. Someone'd be sure to let it slip before long. Twice I almost turned Sally around, my hands itching to get hold of the thieving trash that burnt my home. But then I'd feel Eliza's sleeping head against my back. How could I take care of her and hunt down bushwhackers too? She had to eat, had to have a place to sleep. Besides, I had no weapon. What was one thirteen-year-old boy against a dozen murdering wild men?

I hoped those Rebels would get what they deserved. The Union army hung bushwhackers. Trouble was, the Yankees had lost big barely three weeks ago up at Lexington. Now the Union army was busy chasing Price's men south, and I might have to go clear up to Iowa before I'd find a Union camp. Once I got that far, I had a mind never to set foot in Missouri again.

So I dug a hole in my soul and buried my hatred way down deep. It grew up inside me like corn-choking pigweed, and I had no strength to hoe it out.

Each day as Eliza rode behind me on Sally, she hugged the vegetable sack and rested her head on my back. Sparrows scolded us from low bushes and clumps of grass as we passed by. I thought how they ought to have flown away south by now; a sharp, stinging wind had started up, blowing down from the north. It cut into my eyes and bit my bare toes.

We pushed on, eating the vegetables raw as we went, not wanting to take time to stop and build a fire. Eliza cracked open the green pumpkin and gave me half, but after chewing on its flesh and its gray-green seeds, our guts felt all cramped and sore. What with running off into the trees and squatting every few minutes, we hardly made time. By my reckoning we'd covered close to ninety miles, what with all the backtracking we'd done by sticking close to the river. Fifty long miles still lay between us and the Iowa border.

Now and then a cottontail rabbit shot out from the brush and dashed across the trail into the fields. How I ached to catch one and roast it up, but as I had no gun, nor any knife to skin it with, I let the cottontails be.

Each nightfall I led Sally down through the trees to the creek. She drank her fill and I fed her some oats. Judging by the way she started looking around for more just as soon as she'd finished off what I gave her, I figured we'd better make good time. What was left wouldn't hold her more than three days, if that.

On our ninth day out, Eliza wasn't hungry. She gave me her noontime carrot, saying she just wanted to rest, then she slept through the whole afternoon's ride, her head bobbing against my shoulder blades.

"You start gatherin' wood, Eliza," I said that evening as I tethered Sally to a hickory tree. "I'm goin' to soak my feet."

"I don't like to!" she whined, sitting down right where she was and flopping her chin in her hands. "I'm tired, and wood-gatherin's boys' work."

I'd ought to have known she'd carry on like that. She'd never made a bed or swept a room without fussing and bucking at the idea first.

"Now see here," I said. "You'll do as I say and hush up. I'll take none of your lazy whinin'!"

She wrinkled up her nose and pressed her lips together till they turned white. "You ain't my pa!"

"No, but I'm all you got right now," I said. "If Pa were here he'd be scoutin' around for a good long willow whip."

"Ma wouldn't."

She was right, there. Ma always went easy on Eliza, and it made my pa mad as a fighting cock. He was always after Ma to bring that girl to heel and get her to do her share of the work, but Ma wouldn't, on account of she had peculiar ideas about raising girls. "She's got a lifetime of bone-wearing work to look forward to, Ezra," she'd say, "and I can't see making her run headlong into it yet. I'm going to see to it she has the childhood I never had."

Well, Ma had had her way, mostly. But if we were going to make it all the way to Iowa I needed Eliza's hands and feet as well as my own.

"Get up!" I shouted, feeling my face turn hot. I bent down and grabbed up an old dry hickory stick laying at my feet. It made a nice whistling sound when I swung it through the air a time or two. Eliza got to her feet. She shot me an angry look while she backed around me toward the riverbed, careful to keep her face between me and her backside.

"Go on, get to work!" I ordered once more for good measure. When she was out of sight I tossed the stick down again, marking its place in my mind in case I needed to use it later.

Sitting cross-legged on the bank, I unwrapped my bandages and pulled each foot up to look it over. A good many of the cuts were scabbed over and starting to heal, but some of them oozed all sticky and white where the glass had dug in too deep for me to pick it out. There was nothing for me to do but soak my feet in the creek and scrub my bandages as clean as I could, hanging them to dry on branches till morning. Meanwhile I walked bow-legged on the outside edges of my feet and thanked God I had Sally to do most of my walking for me.

We started up a small fire with the piece of flint I carried in my pocket. I didn't like to let it burn long for fear of being seen, so as soon as we'd roasted a couple of corn ears I put it out. Eliza barely nibbled her corn before handing me the cob. "You eat it, Jacob. I ain't hungry."

I grabbed it and took three greedy bites before stopping myself and giving her a good long look. "What's wrong with you, Eliza? You're always hungry."

She yawned and rubbed her eyes. "I'm just tired, that's all." She shivered, hugging herself tight, then flopped her head down on her pulled-up knees. Before lying down to sleep, we yanked up fistfuls of prairie grass and spread it over ourselves. Though the wind had died down some, the air had gone colder, turning our ears and noses red and numbing our fingers.

"Guess Indian summer's gone for good," I whispered as I curled up close to Eliza beneath our grass blanket. She didn't answer, just coughed a little and shivered. I recollected how she'd sat quiet as a barn cat all through supper, and most of the day, for that matter. "Guess this journey's worn her out like it has me," I thought as sleep came on fast.

Something startled me in the night. Eliza was shaking hard, like she was cold, but when I touched her arm it burnt my fingers like a hot kindling stick. At sunup I cooled her face with creek water, then heaved her up onto Sally. Sick or well, I saw no purpose in sitting still, not when one more day's ride would get us closer to Iowa.

Eliza burnt and shivered behind me all morning long. We crossed a railroad track that I figured must be the one running between Hannibal and St. Joseph. By noontime the ground began to rise up and dip down, turning into grassy hills that stretched away both east and west as far as I could see. The southbound breeze picked up again. Dark gray clouds twisted together and unwound as they rolled above us; here and there a patch of late corn shivered in the biting wind.

By midafternoon Eliza felt no cooler to my touch, though I'd stopped to give her drink and wipe her down with water five times by then.

Once again I turned off the trail toward the creek. I pulled Eliza off the horse and lay her down beneath an elm tree. Two ears of corn were all that was left in the apron sack. With a sharp stone from the creek bed I scraped the corn off the cobs, collecting the sweet white pulp and the bright yellow juice in my cupped hand.

"Eliza!" I shook her by the shoulder. "Eliza, you got to eat!" She moaned and shook her head. "Please, Eliza!" With one arm I lifted her head, then tipped my hand till the raw corn mush ran out into her mouth. Thrashing from side to side, she let it dribble over her chin and down her neck.

"It hurts," she croaked, clawing at her throat.

I felt her forehead. It was hotter than a smoking matchstick. "Then drink somethin'!" I cried, racing to the creek. Scooping up water into my trembling hands, I hurried back to where she lay and knelt down beside her. "Drink, Eliza. Please drink," I begged, dribbling some onto her dry, cracked lips. She jerked her head away, flailing an arm and sending the water sloshing out of my hand. "Dear God," I whispered. "She won't even take drink!"

My eyes and nose began to burn with coming tears, but I fought hard to keep them back. "Oh Lord, I've got to get us out of Missouri! I can't fight sickness too!" My voice trailed up into the sky and disappeared like smoke from a dying fire. A cold wind shook the trees, sending yellow leaves falling on my head.

I wiped my hand on my pants and got to my feet. Stumbling down to the water's edge, I grabbed up an old, dead stick and hurled it with all my might across the creek. It hit the trunk of a big old buckeye tree growing right on the bank, bouncing off into the water with a splash even I could barely hear.

After drying my eyes with my shirtsleeve, I sat watching the dead leaves swirling away south on the water. By the time that tree's shadow grew long enough to reach me on the opposite bank, I'd made my peace with what had to be done. My sister needed help, and I couldn't give it to her by myself. I crawled to the river's edge and drank before climbing back up the bank. I got Eliza onto my shoulder and hoisted her onto the saddle, where she slumped over Sally's neck like a rag doll. Then I led Sally up through the trees and back onto the trail before climbing up behind Eliza.

Night was coming on fast, and my belly growled with hunger. Pushing on northward, I scouted the naked hills for any sign of living folks. It'd been a good long while since I'd laid eyes on a cornfield, and I began to wonder if I might ought to turn around and make for the last farm I'd passed about three miles back. The frosty wind sliced through my shirt and turned my skin to goose flesh. My ears ached with the cold, but I kept on going until the Locust curved around just ahead of me.

"If there's nothin' in sight beyond that bend I'll turn around," I told myself, though the thought of hauling my sister all that way back again made me feel sick inside.

By the time I rounded that curve the sun was halfway down, its dying light falling on a plowed field stretching down the west side of a hill. "Thank God," I sighed. Someone lived nearby.

I steered Sally off the trail toward the field's edge. As we topped the hill, a lone farmhouse came into sight, its windows afire with the last red light of sundown. A low, squatty barn stood next to it, and beyond them both a road snaked its way over the hills into the darkness. Sally edged up the field till we stood even with the house. As the sun sank, the fiery windows turned to black. No light burned in them. There was no sign of a living soul on the place.

A hard knot swelled up in my throat. "Giddap!" I cried, kicking Sally's flanks harder than I needed to, aiming for the road. We'd nearly reached it when I yanked her to a sudden stop.

Down the road, the black shadow of a wagon rose up against the darkening sky, growing bigger as it rolled toward me. I could just make out the figure of a lone driver on the seat as the wagon turned toward the dark house.

The wagon creaked and bounced up the rutted drive toward the barn. Clucking softly to Sally, I turned her toward a thick-trunked walnut tree with low-hanging branches that stood between the field and the house. Safe in its shadow, I slid off the saddle and watched the driver jump down off the wagon seat. The rustle of a woman's skirts and the whistle-snort of a mule carried on the wind, and I heard the woman murmur something to the animal as she unhitched him. A dog came trotting from somewhere out back of the barn, running circles around the woman and yapping hello.

The woman pulled open the barn doors and led the mule inside, stroking his muzzle and humming softly. Before long she came out carrying a bucket and crossed the yard to the back of the house, with the dog close at her heels. A faint clanking noise and a splash sounded from beyond the house, then she returned to the barn with the bucket and disappeared inside. She'd been in there no more than two minutes when a screeching yowl shot up somewhere over by the wagon. I nearly jumped out of my skin, but had enough sense to grab onto Sally's head and hold it down before she pitched Eliza off.

"I'm a-comin', Jimmy!" the woman called over her shoulder as she closed and latched the barn door. Her dark figure moved to the wagon box and picked up a small, wiggling bundle wrapped in white. Cradling it close, she crossed the yard to the house and started up the steps.

Just then Sally yanked her head up hard and let loose with a loud whinny. I crouched down behind the walnut trunk, watching and waiting. The woman stopped short, half turning on the steps, listening. Then she hurried on up and into the house.

The dog stayed on the porch. He lifted his nose and cocked his head, trying to sniff us out. Growling low down in his throat, he inched his way along the edge of the top step. His body tensed. Then, with one mighty leap, he bounded down and raced toward us, yelping like mad. I hugged Sally's neck and squeezed my eyes shut, bracing against the dog's attack. It never came. When I opened my eyes I saw that a lamp had been lit and was shining out from the door of the house. The dog paced back and forth at the edge of its glow, snarling but coming no further. Behind him stood the woman in the lit doorway, a shotgun in her hand.

"Who's there?" she called above the dog's growling. She moved slowly down the steps. "Hush, Calhoun!" she hollered, grabbing hold of the scruff of his neck with her free hand. "I said, who is it?"

My heart flopped in my chest like a fish on a riverbank. I wanted to answer her, to tell her we needed help, but my mouth wouldn't budge.

"I ain't got a horse, nor anything worth stealin'!" she shouted above the dog's growling. "Whoever you are, you'd best move on before I shoot!"

It was high time to speak out. On shaking legs, and holding on to Eliza with one hand, I led Sally forward through the walnut branches.

"It's just us, ma'am," I called out, my voice all atremble. "Just me and my sister, that's all. Don't shoot!"

She lifted her gun and aimed it in our direction. She stood quiet a minute, then spoke more softly, "What? Children?"

The woman stood in the lit doorway,
a shotgun in her hand.

Coming closer, she looked us over as best she could in the thin lamplight. I'd never been one to like being gawked at. When I tried to pull myself up tall, a bone-slicing pain tore through my feet. I hung my head and wiped my nose on my shirtsleeve. Calhoun strained toward us, yelping and yawling till she yanked him hard and shushed him again.

"Are you alone?" she asked.

"Yes ma'am. My sister's sick; she's took fever."

The woman hesitated a moment. She glanced back toward her house, then back at us with her forehead all wrinkled up. Finally she lowered the gun to her side, saying, "Then you'd best stable your horse and come in."

Maggie

Her name was Margaret Wilkinson Canaday, though she said most folk called her just plain Maggie. She was tall and lean, with hardworking hands and a sharp-boned face. Her lips fit together in a hard, straight line, and I might have feared her just a little if she hadn't been so gentle with my sister.

After stirring up embers and laying kindling on top, Maggie brought cool water and wiped Eliza down. She dug around in a cupboard and pulled out a dust-covered bottle. "Quinine for fever..." she said, thinking aloud, "and let me see..." She hurried to her kitchen fire and brewed up some kind of sweet-smelling tea.

Blowing the dust off the quinine bottle, she forced a spoonful of the liquid down Eliza's throat, followed by three spoonfuls of tea. "Lilac tea brings on a sweat," she told me as she wiped Eliza's chin with a corner of her apron. "Sweatin's good. It'll cool her down." Then Maggie lifted my sister in strong arms and carried her up a dark, narrow stairway. Halfway up she turned to me, nodding that I should follow.

"Bring up the lamp, boy."

In a tiny attic room, Maggie lay Eliza on an old bed with a worn-out cornhusk tick. She carefully undressed her. Then, pulling a bed linen from a small cupboard, she shook it out and spread it on the tick. I rolled Eliza's limp body first one way, then another while Maggie smoothed the sheet beneath her. After covering my sister with a quilt, Maggie held her finger to her lips and turned to go, her long shadow flickering up the wall and across the ceiling. I sat down beside my sister.

"Leave her be now," said Maggie.

"No ma'am. I'll stay right here. Thanks just the same."

She set her hands on her hips. "Young man...just what is your name?"

"Jacob Knight."

"Well, Jacob Knight, your feet need attendin' to. There ain't no one here but me who can do it. Now get on down those stairs." She stooped to pick up the lamp and walked out, leaving me in pitch darkness.

Sliding my arm across the bed, I found Eliza's hand and gave it a squeeze. "I ain't goin' far," I whispered. Then I let myself down the stairs on my hindquarters to spare my feet.

I couldn't keep myself from groaning when Maggie pressed a boiled rag into the soles of my feet and dug out the deep glass shards with a sewing needle.

"Hush up, now," she whispered. "You'll wake Jimmy."

Turning my head to where the baby lay in a cradle near the fire, I bit deep into my lower lip and squeezed my eyes shut tight, hoping to God she wouldn't see me bawl. But when she chopped up an onion and washed my wounds in its sharp, stinging juice, I couldn't help myself.

"Shhh now, Jacob," she murmured. "The worst is done, and you can start to mend." Maggie tore up two clean dishcloths and wound them tight around my feet. She helped me over to the hearth rug and sat me down, for by now her baby was fretting and fussing and hollering for his supper.

Maggie picked him up and sank into a rocking chair to put him to her breast. Jimmy snorted and kicked his strong little legs while he ate, clenching and opening his fat fists, while his ma leaned her tired head back onto the rocker.

"I expect your sister will be all right," she said, closing her eyes. "But I'll watch her through the night, just the same."

For the first time since the night the bushwhackers came I felt my load lightened, like when someone comes alongside and shares the lifting of a full water bucket. Tears came, stinging my tired, dusty eyes. Trying to hide them, I lay down on the floor facing the fire, but a great choking sob burst out and I covered my whole face with my dirty hands. Calhoun wandered out of a dark corner of the house, his nails clicking across the wooden floor, and sank down at the rocker's side. With a heavy sigh he dropped his muzzle onto his paws.

"Don't cry, Jacob," murmured Maggie. "This war's ripped many a family in two. I expect yours ain't the first, nor will it be the last."

I looked up, startled, wondering how she knew, for I hadn't told her any more than my name.

Opening her eyes, she looked not at me, but deep into the flames. "You been run off your land, Jacob?"

"Yes ma'am," I said, sniffing hard and wiping my nose with my shirtsleeve. "Rebel bushwhackers done it. They burnt down our house and barn. Took all our livestock too. Eliza and I ran off, and now we can't find our folks."

She lifted little Jimmy to her shoulder, nuzzling her cheek against his fuzzy head. The steady creaking of her rocker echoed through the still, dark house. After a minute or two, the creaking stopped. When I looked up I saw her eyes shut tight and her jaw set firm.

"Well," she finally sighed, "I reckon you'll need some supper."

~

I could hardly get the cornbread into my mouth fast enough. It crumbled and bounced all over the table and onto my lap, so I fumbled for the crumbs as best I could and ate them too.

"Slow down, child!" scolded Maggie, one corner of her mouth turning up a little. She crouched by the fire, frying up salt pork in a spider skillet. Her hair was coming loose from the knot at the back of her head, glowing red-gold against the flames. Spearing the sizzling meat with a fork, she dropped it onto a plate and set it down before me on the table.

Dressed in butternut-dyed homespun, Maggie stood with chapped, raw-knuckled hands on her hips, watching me eat. Her voice was young, but her forehead had deep furrows dug into it, like she'd known hard times. She wasn't pretty like a lady in a picture print, just honest and simple, and I felt safe in her presence. When I glanced up at her I shamed to see pity on her face, so I fixed my eyes back on my supper.

When Maggie had fed me she went back to work on Eliza. Fetching up a carrot from the cellar, she passed it over a grater and spread it out on a clean dishrag. Then she folded it over and dipped both rag and carrot into boiling water. "There's nothing like a carrot poultice for healing a sore throat," she assured me. "Now don't worry about your sister, Jacob. I'll tie this rag around her neck. In the morning she'll feel better, though it may take some time before she's back to her old self." The sweet carrot smell filled the house and tickled my nose as I watched her carry it upstairs. When she came down again she brought a worn-out quilt and a small feather pillow.

"You know it's ague season, don't you, Jacob?" she said. "Tomorrow she'll shake, next day she'll be hot...and her throat's worse off than I thought. You did right to come to my door." She tossed me the bedding. "You sleep here by the fire tonight. I'll keep watch upstairs; that's where Jimmy and I sleep."

When I lay down, Calhoun flopped down beside me, warming me from behind while the fire warmed me in front. For the first time I saw he was a brown-spotted bird dog, and I smiled a little, thinking how he'd been fit to tear me to pieces not three hours before. Curling up beneath my blanket, I felt the fire's warmth spreading across my face. My thoughts turned back toward Eliza. Our family had known the ague before; two summers ago, Ma'd taken to her bed with it. "Malarial fevers," the doctor had pronounced when he rode out from Boonesboro to attend to her, and I recalled that he'd given her quinine, just like Maggie'd given Eliza tonight. "Oh God," I prayed, "I'm sorry. Maybe I pushed Eliza too hard these last nine days, expected too much of her." But even as I confessed my wrongs, I knew I'd done right. Pressing north toward Iowa was the only thing I could have done.

Next morning, Maggie helped me up the stairs. She dug deep into an oak chest at the foot of her bed and pulled out a small pair of shoes and a faded yellow dress. Shaking the dress out good, she held it up in the window's light. "I reckon I was near fourteen years old when I wore this, but no matter. I'll cut it down. Your sister could do with another dress." She tossed it across the bed, where Jimmy lay gurgling and spluttering on his belly, his strong arms holding himself up while his head wobbled all over the place.

Maggie turned her eyes on me then, letting them wander from my sooty hair down my filthy, bug-smeared pants to my bare toes sticking out of the bloody bandages.

Feeling my face flush hot, I drew myself up as tall and straight as I could. "We had the second biggest farm in our township!" I blurted out. "Pa built us a new house three years ago, twice as big as this one here—and we had near fifteen hogs to sell this winter!"

She kept on staring at my toes like she hadn't heard a word of it. "It ain't no shame to run barefoot in Indian summer, Jacob," she said, "but winter's knockin' on the door. When those feet are healed, you'll want shoes."

"There'll be shoes aplenty in Iowa, where I'm goin'," I told her. She looked at me a little bit surprised, then pointed to a corner of the room. Against the wall leaned a pair of boots, split-seamed and worn down in the heels. Clearly they'd been made for bigger feet than mine. A single strand of spider's web stretched from the top of one boot to the wall.

"They'll have to do till we can afford better," she declared.

I didn't tell her then what I was thinking: I had no plans to stay on her shabby little farm any longer than I had to.

"As for clothes...." she continued, crossing to a tall chest of drawers and opening the top one, "Clem's a tall man." She pulled out a pair of brown, homespun trousers and coat. "But I'll cut them down." Fishing out a pair of suspenders and a shirt, she tossed them on top of Eliza's dress and shoes.

"Who's Clem?" I asked.

She didn't answer, only looked me over again with a sharp eye. "Clean clothes need a clean body to hang on!"

That afternoon she boiled water and filled a wooden tub for me in the kitchen. She lay a towel on a nearby chair, then left me to myself.

"Wash your toes, but don't get the bandages wet!" she called from the front room.

"Yes ma'am," I answered, wondering just how on God's earth I was supposed to do that.

"You need help, Jacob?"

"No ma'am, and you don't come in here, either! A man wants privacy at bath time."

A shadow fell over the kitchen floor, and there stood Maggie in the doorway with her hands covering her eyes. She flung a wad of clean clothes on the floor in my direction.

"Well, I'm glad to hear you consider yourself a man, Jacob," she said, bending down the corners of her mouth almost like she was trying to keep from laughing. "As long as you're on this farm, you'll have to wear a man's clothes. Can you do a man's chores?"

"Yes ma'am," I said, sinking myself as far down into the tub as I could, in case she peeked.

"Good!" She turned away, finally leaving me in peace.

When I'd scrubbed and dressed, Maggie carried Eliza down and bathed her too. Shaking so hard her teeth clattered, Eliza said nothing, only stared up at Maggie like she'd never seen a grown woman before. "It's all right," I whispered to her when Maggie turned her back to fetch the soap. "Just let her doctor you." Maggie scrubbed Eliza and dried her off, then carried her up to bed again.

"Where are we, Jacob?" Eliza whispered when I hobbled up the stairs to check on her that evening. "I never saw that woman before. That ain't Aunt Lucille, is it?"

"Naw!" I snorted. "Course not. We're still in Missouri."

Eliza lay back on her pillow, rubbing her throat. "Wish we weren't."

"Me too," I said. "But we're gonna get on out of here, quick as we can. Just as soon as you're well."

Next Maggie smeared soft soap all over our filthy clothes, beating and rubbing them hard between her knuckles. I helped her wring them out, then watched her through the window as she spread them over a row of rough, gray-barked hawthorn bushes to dry in the fresh air.

"Who's Clem?" I asked again the next morning, standing still so Maggie could measure where to cut his clothes so they'd fit me. The sleeves of his shirt hung almost to my knees and I thought how I must look like a weasel in a bucket wearing his pants.

She looked up at me with a mouthful of pins, her face gone all white. Then she pulled the pins out slowly, one by one. "Clem's my husband," she answered, sticking the pins right back in her mouth and going on with her work. I decided to keep my questions to myself for a while.

For five long days I sat in Maggie's house, on account of her not letting me go even as far as the front porch in my wrapped-up feet. I told her I wished I could chop some wood for her; she told me to just sit tight and let my feet heal. "You just mind the baby; that's help enough," she said one morning on her way out the back door. Feeling ashamed that she had to feed and water my horse, I sat rocking little Jimmy's cradle and mopping up his spit-up with a rag. She wouldn't even let me go upstairs to see my sister anymore, saying the less I used my feet the quicker they'd mend. But each evening when Maggie served me my bowl of corn mush and milk, and sat down to feed Jimmy, she told me how Eliza was getting on. "That girl's got some fight in her," she reassured me. "Betwixt that and my doctorin', she's mendin' about as well as I could expect."

Sure enough, by the sixth day Eliza's fever broke, and my feet were scabbed over. I decided we ought to be off again, and I told Maggie as much.

"Jacob, winter's comin' on fast, and Eliza ain't fully well," objected Maggie. "The ague hangs on awhile before it finally quits a body. Most likely the fever'll come back again two or three more times 'fore she's rid of it."

"That may be so," I said, holding Jimmy on my lap. He gurgled and slobbered and flapped his arms, and the sweet smell of his skin brought to mind my baby sister, Jerusha. A lump rose in my throat all of a sudden. "But we...well, we've got to try to find our folks."

Maggie crossed the room and looked out the front window. She drummed her fingers against the glass awhile. "Jacob, do you know for sure your folks went up north?"

I sat quiet, my eyes closed. Again I saw the smoke curling up from the ruins of my home, and a deep, cold fear slithered like a snake through my mind. The smothering silence hanging over our farm weighed me down till I could hardly draw breath. Nearly choking, I fought off the memory.

"I reckon I don't," I finally answered.

"And your kinfolks' farm in Iowa. Do you know where it is, exactly?"

"No ma'am, though I know it's somewhere near Iowa City."

She turned back to me, a black shadow against the bright light of the window. "Missouri's full of the war right now, Jacob," she said. "There's bloodlettin' all over these hills, what with Union gangs and bushwhackers and such ridin' around. And horse thieves everywhere! I can't let children loose into such a place."

Jimmy squealed. He curled all his little fingers around one of mine and pulled it up toward his mouth. I bent my finger up and let him chaw on my knuckle a bit, like I used to do with

Jerusha back home. I stared down at his face with a fluttering in my belly, not quite knowing what to say to his mama.

She was right. The Confederacy had its bushwhackers, but the Union had itself some ruffians too. We called them Jayhawkers. They came riding over the border from Kansas, looting and burning and generally doing to the Rebel folk what the Rebel gang had done to us. They weren't like regular Union or Confederate soldiers. Neither side took orders from any general; they had no leaders to speak of. Getting revenge was their only aim, and each side gave as good as it got. The state militia tried hard to keep the peace, but had a hard time of it, what with so few men having joined up.

Pa, for one, didn't like what the Union gangs were doing. He said they were no better than bushwhackers, and they ought to just stay home and let the Union army do its job. Of course I'd always thought my Pa spoke true and right about such things, but lately I'd been wondering. Ever since we got bushwhacked, I felt glad to know that somewhere in Missouri a gang of Jayhawkers was setting fire to a Rebel farm. Well, what did those cursed bushwhackers expect? That they could just run amuck all over Missouri, and not get paid back what they deserved?

Maggie stepped up beside me, putting a hand on my shoulder and fixing her gray eyes on mine. "Wait for spring, Jacob. Could be by then the war'll be done with, and you can go home."

I felt myself trembling all over. What Maggie said was true. Only God knew what dangers we'd run into between here and Iowa. But I was determined to do what I'd set out to do. Clearing my throat, I spoke up as plain and strong as I could. "Just the same, Eliza and I'll be off in the mornin'."

Maggie crossed to the window again and sat down on the sill. Pressing her forehead against the pane, she let out a long sigh. "Well, Jacob. I can't hold you if leavin's what you want."

That night I slept next to my sister on the cornhusk bed. A haversack Maggie'd packed with corn pone and hog jerky waited on the floor next to the bed along with the boots she'd given me. But when dawn came, it brought with it a rain that beat hard against the attic windowpane.

Bundled up in wool blankets, we sat half the morning watching the raindrops dribble down the windows and waiting for it to let up. It never did. At noon I tramped out through freezing wind to the road for a good look at the sky. It stretched out iron gray as far as I could see in every direction. The rain pelted my face with slivers of ice that slid down my neck and under my shirt collar. It beat the hills hard, slapping the last of the black-eyed Susans, swirling down through the grass in muddy rivers. When my hands grew numb and red I went inside to dry off at Maggie's fire.

Darkness fell. The rain fell as hard as ever. Suppertime came and went.

"We'll see about tomorrow," I told Maggie as I ate my corn mush. But later that night, when I climbed beneath the quilt and curled up next to Eliza, I could feel her shaking again with fever. I rolled over on the crackling husk tick and cried myself to sleep.

Squaw Man
Trade

Three more days Eliza burned and shivered in that attic bed. On the fourth day she sat up with color in her cheeks, but by that time I'd come to realize we weren't going anywhere. I guess I'd known all along that Maggie was right about the ague, that a body could suffer with it a good long while once it took hold. I had no business dragging my sister up to Iowa in the cold, and through woods alive with bushwhackers. We'd winter with Maggie; it couldn't be helped. Maggie told me to share Eliza's bed now that she was some better, and to make myself at home up there in her attic.

I still itched to climb on Sally and ride away north, if for no other reason than to escape the whirlwind Missouri had become. Yet Missouri held me prisoner, squeezing its arms tight around my middle, threatening to kill me if I tried to flee. But I'd bide my time. Sooner or later spring would break, and Missouri would loosen its grip.

I comforted myself with the thought that Pa and Ma must surely have reached Aunt Lucille's in Iowa by now. Each night at bedtime Eliza asked me did I think Ma and Pa and Jerusha and Sarah were all right. "Of course they are," I'd tell her. "By this time they're lookin' for us out Lucille's front window."

The rain turned to drizzle and hovered over the hills for most of a week, stopping only to make room for November's first frost. I helped Maggie haul in walnuts and apples and the last of her garden vegetables. I tended the livestock too, pleased to see Sally shut safely away from thieves at night. I knew Pa'd be pleased to know I was taking good care of his horse.

"I'll be plain with you, Jacob," said Maggie one afternoon when we were in the barn sorting apples. "A woman winterin' alone has more than she can handle. I'm obliged to you already for the help you'll be."

"I thank you for lettin' us stay," I said, glancing down at my almost-good-as-new feet. "We're beholden to you for all you've done for us."

I figured then was as good a time as any to ask her what I'd been wondering about ever since I'd come to her farm. "Your husband, Clem. Is he a soldier?"

Maggie threw a rotting apple in the pig's slop bucket. I waited. She threw another and another. "No," she finally answered. "He ain't." And she grabbed up the bucket and made off for the pigpen without another word.

The next morning Maggie braided up Eliza's hair and pinned it to her head. "I always did admire yellow hair," she said. "How I did wish for it as a child!" She dipped her fingers into a washbowl and smoothed down my own brown hair that always stuck out every which way. "But the Lord gave to me red hair like He gave to Jacob brown. I make the best of it, and so must you, boy."

Maggie wrapped herself in a shawl, then bundled Eliza up good and snug. "Fresh air'll do you good, child, now your fever's broke." She pulled a man's Sunday jacket off a wall peg and placed it around my shoulders. "Wrap up tight, Jacob!" Then with Jimmy in her arms, she set out up the drive, careful to walk on the grassy hump between the muddy wheel ruts. Eliza and I trailed behind her, me shuffling slowly in Clem's big boots. Though my feet were all but healed, they were still tender.

Turning left onto the road, she led us a quarter mile or so uphill and down until we came to a store sitting all alone in a draw where two roads crossed. Built right onto it was a log cabin with a half dozen sheep in a split rail pen behind it.

Over the store's door, painted in bright red, were the words Squaw Man Trade, established 1831. Crouched above the lettering, a fierce, painted Indian waved a tomahawk, ready to attack. Next to him I could barely make out the faded words Henry Wilkinson, Proprietor.

A bell jingled as Maggie opened the door and stepped inside. Eliza and I followed her into a dim, spice-smelling room. It looked like most little crossroads stores I'd seen, with shelves crammed all full of molasses, rice, sugar, salt, tea, and spices. Bridle bits and tinware hung from pegs on the walls; stacks of Bibles, playing cards, and almanacs sat gathering dust in a corner. Piled high on the long counter were iron pots and baskets full of needles, thimbles, and spools of thread.

"Ma!" Maggie called out.

A curtain in the wall behind the counter rippled, then drew aside. Out stepped a lanky, white-haired woman with a clay pipe hanging from her lips. She looked me up and down with squeezed-up eyes, popping them open wide when she caught sight of Eliza.

"Lord have mercy, Margaret! She's a-wearin' yer dress! How'd she get it?"

"I gave it to her, Ma," answered Maggie. "Her name's Eliza. This here is her brother, Jacob."

"Eliza and Jacob who?" croaked the old woman, looking down her nose at us.

"Knight!" I spoke up.

She closed her eyes and sucked her pipe a minute. "Knight? I don't recall anyone in these hills with that name."

"They ain't from Linn County, Ma," explained Maggie, lowering her voice. "They just lately arrived from down south...seekin' shelter."

The old woman snatched the pipe out of her mouth. She blasted smoke out one side and pressed her lips together so hard her chin nearly touched the tip of her nose. "Filthy Secesh bush-whackers!" she spat. "Well, ye're welcome here, for we're Union folk like yerselves." She pulled aside the curtain and motioned for us to follow.

The sweet, heavy smell of tobacco slapped me full in the face as I stepped through the doorway onto the oak plank floor. It mingled with the gamey smell of a stew, bubbling in a fireplace that ran along one whole wall of the room. Squares of light fell onto the dark cabin floor through two tiny windows cut into the log walls. A hollowed-out corncob stuffed with an oil-soaked wick burned on a table next to where I stood, giving out the only other light in the place. As my eyes got used to the darkness, I peeked at each corner of the room.

A log post bed took up one whole corner, draped over with a big black bearskin. Another bearskin stretched across one wall, next to a dress and bonnet and a man's Sunday suit hang-ing on pegs. In another corner stood a floor loom beside baskets heaped high with wool.

"Come on in and set!" Maggie's ma invited, so we sat right down at her table. She scooped out steaming bowls of venison potpie and set them down in front of us. "Will ye have molasses on yer corn pone?" she asked.

"Yes ma'am," I answered, sucking the delicious steam up into my nose.

"Yes'm," echoed Eliza.

Maggie's ma stuck her long fingers right down into the molasses jar, then dribbled the sticky black syrup across our corn-bread. I held down my surprise, but Eliza gawked wide-eyed.

"Our ma would have a fit if we tried such a thing at her table!" she blurted out.

"Hush, Eliza!" I whispered, pinching her in the ribs. "Thank you, ma'am."

"I'm Susannah," Maggie's ma replied, licking her fingers with a great big smack.

Just then the front door of the cabin banged open and a burst of light shot in. On the threshold stood a lean, tall figure of a man, a rifle in one hand. A pack of hounds circled his feet, barking and howling and jumping up at a brace of dead bob-white quails hanging over his shoulder.

"Pa!" cried Maggie with a big smile. "You got you some partridges!"

The hunter slammed the door on his dogs. He limped to the table and thumped the birds down on one end of it, making our plates jump and clatter; specks of dust floated up into the windows' light. Standing stock-still, he sized up Eliza and me. A lump of dry corn pone caught like a rock in my throat. I fidgeted in my chair, wiping the crumbs from my lips with a jittery hand.

Maggie rested her hand on my shoulder. "Pa, this here is Jacob Knight and his sister Eliza, lately arrived from down south. They're needin' shelter, so they'll 'bide with me this winter." She looked down at us. "Jacob and Eliza, make acquaintance with my pa, Captain Henry Wilkinson."

Captain Wilkinson stretched out an arm toward me. When I stood up and stuck my hand out to meet his, he grabbed hold, squeezing until I nearly cried out. He nodded at Eliza, who sat looking foolish with her mouth open and a piece of cornbread hanging out. When I kicked her she clapped her mouth shut, mumbling a little and looking back down into her potpie. Taking my seat, I set to eating again, but I kept one eye on Captain Wilkinson just the same.

His cheekbones stuck out sharp on either side of his hawk-beak nose. Eyes the color of wild prairie violets lay buried in his red, leathery face, and a thin white scar ran from his left ear to the corner of his mouth. Wild white hair grew thick all over his head except for the top. He wore an old-fashioned buckskin hunting shirt, and from his belt hung a shot pouch, knife, and tomahawk.

Captain Henry turned to his daughter, taking off a squirrel-skin cap with the feet dangling down the side. "Maggie, I saw the sheriff today on the Linneus road. He brought word of yer husband."

"Clem?" Maggie whispered, going pale. She hoisted Jimmy over to her other hip and steadied herself. "What word, Pa?"

Henry Wilkinson just looked at her a minute. A kind of ornery smile came into his face as he propped his flintlock against the wall, then stumped over to a water bucket near the front door and drew himself a drink. We all watched him drain the tin cup dry, smacking his lips and wiping his mouth with the back of his hand. Slowly he eased himself into one of the chairs at the table, his favored leg stuck out straight before him.

"Tell me, Pa!" begged Maggie.

"Seems Clem's been a-tearin' up train tracks and blowin' up bridges. Seems he's been a thorn in the side of the Union army hereabouts, generally. Now a Union regiment's set up camp over at Linneus. The provost marshal nailed up a wanted poster two days ago with Clem's name on it."

Maggie shut her mouth tight. She turned and walked slowly to the loom in the corner and leaned her forehead against it.

"Well, I say keep a lookout!" the old man continued. "'Cause Clem Canaday's likely to turn up here one day soon! Yes sir, winter'll drive him home and then we'll watch him pay for all his wrongdoin'!"

"Now there ye go spoutin' nonsense!" spat Susannah. She crossed the room and lifted her grandbaby out of Maggie's arms. "Clem won't dare to show his face hereabouts, after what he done. We all know he took the oath! I reckon he knows by now the Union army hangs bushwhackers...and oath-breakers."

Henry stomped his boot hard on the plank floor. "Maybe so, but wouldn't it be just like Clem to try to sneak back home again? Try to pick up his plow, and carry on like he ain't done nothin' wrong? I curse the day Maggie married that Rebel!"

Maggie drew a deep breath. "Now, Pa."

"He run off and left ye, didn't he?" shouted Henry. "Up and turned Rebel, didn't he, even after he swore loyalty to the Union? Burnt down Asa Wheeler's barn, stole his horse, then run off with a band of bushwhackers and left ye to starve!"

"I'm gettin' by, Pa."

"And ye with a new baby! And now two extry mouths to feed."

Maggie jerked herself out of shadows. She rushed to Susannah and snatched back her baby. "I said we'll get by, Pa! Jacob and Eliza'll earn their keep. When winter's done, the war may be done too. Then Clem'll come home."

Captain Henry heaved himself to his feet so fast his chair tipped and clattered to the floor. Hobbling circles around the room, he shook an angry fist in the air. "Why, I'd join up iffen they'd let me. I'd wear the blue and fight as fierce as any man for the Union. I took the oath and I'd as soon die as break it!"

Susannah let out a sharp cackle. "Listen to the old man!" she screeched, waving her pipe in the air with a clawlike hand. "The Federals got no use for an old cripple like ye, so set down!"

With Jimmy in one arm, Maggie strode toward her pa. She reached up with her free hand and grabbed hold of his balled-up fist. "We need you here, Pa," she said quietly. "You got to hunt for us, or we'll never get enough meat this winter 'less we eat up our livestock. Clem's been gone four months now. I reckon he ain't comin' back."

The old man opened his mouth to speak but shut it again, bending his ear toward the cabin door. A far-off rumbling of wagon wheels grew louder until we could hear the snap of a whip and a shrill voice yelling "Haw!" When the rumbling turned to close-up creaking, the dogs on the porch began to howl. Henry limped to the door, flung it open, and gave his hounds a shove with his lame foot.

"Hush up!" he barked.

I jumped up and followed him onto the porch. A tired old mule pulling a farm wagon came clopping down the road, whipped on by a lone woman in the driver's seat. Behind her in the wagon box, four dirty-faced children sat wedged between a pile of furniture, pots and pans, and all kinds of belongings. They rocked back and forth with the wagon's jolting, staring out at us with eyes all hollow. The biggest one, a red-haired girl sitting on a butter churn, covered her face and turned her head away from us as she passed by.

No sooner had that wagon rolled away than another followed. Another came, then another, driven by women, tight-lipped and grim-faced. Each wagon box was full to bursting with children and household goods. Susannah, Maggie, and Eliza stepped outside, the two women counting the wagons in hushed voices. There were fourteen in all, and no sign of a grown man among them.

A black-haired boy who looked to be about fifteen drove the last wagon. He pulled himself up tall in the driver's seat and flapped the reigns importantly. Then he peeked over at me to see if I'd noticed.

"Where you goin'?" I hollered.

"Don't know!" he called back. "We're lookin' for the Union army. Rebels burnt down our house. Took my pa!" He was gone before he could say more. I watched his mussed-up head of hair till it sank down below the crest of the hill.

"Filthy Rebel bushwhackers!" muttered Susannah through the pipe in her teeth.

"How many wagons is that now, Pa, in all?" asked Maggie.

"That makes sixty-seven this month, near as I can count. Those cussed Confederates are clearin' out whole counties southwest of here." Henry stood with his arms crossed, his head turned toward the hill the wagons had disappeared behind. "Yessir, the Yankees'll hang Clem good and high when they get their hands on him."

"Bah! He's smart enough not to come back and let himself be hung!" scoffed Susannah.

Henry shot his hunter's eyes along the hilltops to where a buzzard hawk floated in a silent circle. He shook his head, then turned back to his wife and pointed a long, bony finger in her face. "He'll be back. Ye mark my words!"

That night Eliza's voice came trembling out from underneath her side of the quilt. "He's comin' here, ain't he, Jacob?"

"Who?" I asked, although I knew good and well who.

"The bushwhacker. Is he goin' to burn us out of here, too?"

I flung the cover off my face and rolled over onto one elbow, exasperated. "He ain't goin' to burn down his own house, Eliza! Now hush up and go to sleep."

The wind screeched and hollered in the framework above us while we lay quiet a spell. Then Eliza lifted her head off her pillow. "You ain't goin' to let him hurt me, are you, Jacob?"

"Naw," I said. "Naw, I ain't goin' to let him touch a hair on your head."

She lay quiet a minute. "You still plannin' to take us up to Iowa?"

"Just as soon as spring comes," I said. "Now go to sleep."

She pulled the quilt up over her chin and turned toward the wall, leaving me alone with the wind and the darkness.

So Clem Canaday was a bushwhacker and an oath-breaker. Well, I knew all about the oath. After the war broke out last spring and the Union army moved into Missouri, some of its officers wanted men to swear loyalty to the Union. Sometimes they made life hard for those who wouldn't, seizing their land or throwing them in jail. My pa being a Union man, it seemed only natural for him to swear himself true to the U.S. government. I rode into the Yankee camp with him to watch him take the oath before the provost marshal. But that same day, a whole mess of folk we knew to be Secesh lined up to take the oath too.

Dirty liars, Pa called them when he told Ma about it, but Ma had shushed him. "They have to live same as we do, Ezra," she scolded. "I can't say as I blame them for their lies." She had a point, but so did Pa. Not long after, we started hearing tales of civilian folk taking up arms against the Union, even after they'd taken the oath. They lay in wait to ambush the Union soldiers whenever they could, cutting off their supplies and attacking their posts. Well, the Federals weren't going to tolerate that one bit. They let it be known that any Missourian caught oathbreaking could expect to be hung, and quickly too.

I got out of bed and crept to the window on bare feet. The cold floor sent chills up my legs beneath the long nightshirt I wore—Clem's nightshirt. I rubbed steam off the window and pressed my eye to the glass, watching clouds catch the moon, then turn it loose again.

"Bushwhacker," I whispered, my breath making new steam on the window. What if he came back to his farm? Such a one wasn't fit to be Maggie's husband, didn't belong here in the house with little Jimmy. Maggie was a good woman. What was she doing hitched up with a barn-burning Confederate? She'd been kind to take us in, but I'd rather die than winter in the same quarters as a Rebel outlaw. Clem Canaday's low-down kind had taken our family away from Eliza and me. My eyes grew wet with a sudden sadness, and I crawled back into bed. I lay there awhile, thinking of my ma, pa, and sisters; of the farm I'd lived on since I could remember. A gnawing hunger burnt my insides as I reached my hands out into the blackness.

"Ma!" I cried softly, longing to feel her straightening my hair the way she always did before Sunday meeting. And though it had always bothered me to no end, I wanted to hear little Sarah's chatter, to hear Jerusha fuss and kick in her cradle. To sit close beside my pa on the wagon seat again.

Susannah said Clem was too smart to come back and let himself be hung, and I guessed she was probably right. But a man who had run another man's family off their land and burnt down their home ought to pay for what he'd done. Most likely I'd never have the satisfaction of seeing the thieving scum that burnt my home get their due, but Clem Canaday had bush-whacked a Union farm just like they did. I didn't know how, but I knew one thing just as sure as I lived. If that bushwhacker came slinking back home while I was there, I'd have my revenge.

Ruins on the Hillside

M aggie's farm was a small one. She didn't own but one cow, eight hogs, a few chickens scratching around outside her kitchen door, and an old brown cotton mule. Each day for as long as the snow held off, I turned the cow, the mule, and Sally out to pasture so they could get their fill of the grass and the fresh air.

Henry'd named the mule Lazarus, after someone Jesus raised from the dead. I found out why one morning when Eliza shook me awake. An awful ruckus was coming from the barn. Huddled together in the dingy light, we heard a rattling and banging so loud it was like to shake the whole barn down. An awful cursing and a high whistling snort rose up from the yard, making me jump from the bed and race to the window. Seeing the barn door open, I made straight for Maggie's bedroom door across the hall. I knocked hard.

"Maggie! There's someone in the barn!" I pressed my ear to the wood and heard the noisy spluttering Jimmy made when Maggie fed him.

"It's only Pa, Jacob, goin' to town for supplies. Never you mind."

I rubbed my eyes, then went back to my window. Eliza stumbled out of bed and joined me there, shivering. Sure enough, old Henry finally appeared in the barn doorway, yanking so hard on the mule's lead he'd have fallen clean over if he'd suddenly let go. He pulled the mule forward two steps, then quick as a lame man could, he jumped behind Lazarus and slapped the mule's rump hard. Lazarus jerked his head from side to side, making as if to sit down right there, but Henry planted his two hands on that mule's behind, pushing with all his might. Then, before the ornery animal could kick out with his hind legs, Henry hopped on his good leg up front of Lazarus again, planted his feet firm, and pulled, not giving up an inch of ground. By and by he managed to hitch Lazarus up to Maggie's wagon, but by then it looked as if his white hair was all stuck to his head with sweat. Climbing up onto the wagon seat, he caught his breath a minute before flapping the reins and setting off up the drive.

"Poor Pa!" a voice said from behind me.

I spun around, startled half out of my wits. Maggie had crept quietly into our room, with Jimmy in her arms.

"That old mule's as sweet as honeycake with me," she said, "but he never does go willingly with Pa. He says gettin' that mule up and goin's like tryin' to wake the dead. He figured Lazarus was about as fittin' a name as any other."

I felt sorry for Henry and told Maggie so. I offered to lend him Sally but Maggie shook her head no.

"You'd best leave a fine horse like Sally home nowadays, Jacob," she replied. "No sense temptin' horse thieves."

Maggie's fields had lain fallow all through the last growing season, excepting one field of corn her husband Clem had planted in the spring. Its dried-out stalks stood naked in the field, for Henry and Susannah had already helped Maggie pick off the ears and load them into a sheltered crib to dry. It wasn't near as much as we used to bring in on our farm—it barely filled the crib—but even so it needed shucking so we could use it for our winter's food.

On shucking day, Henry hobbled up the drive with a fiddle strapped to his back and Susannah at his side. We waited for them out at the corncrib, all wrapped up in scarves and gloves and watching our breath cloud up in the air.

As the old man drew near I could see he was fit to burst with some kind of happy news. He grinned wide and stuck his chest out so far his coat buttons nearly burst.

"There's been more fightin' here in Missouri!" was his greeting. "Jest two days ago!"

"Where?" cried Maggie. "Close by?"

"Naw. Down Kentucky way. Some Union fella named Ulysses Grant shook up the Rebels down there. Burned their camp!"

"Hallelujah!" I clapped my frozen hands. "What then?"

"Aw, hang me iffen the Rebs didn't chase the Yankees back to where they come from." Henry shook his head, disgusted. "But it does a body good to know the Rebels got hit hard. Iffen there's one thing I can't abide, it's the thought of Confederate soldiers prowlin' around Missouri!" Henry spat on the ground.

"And I can't abide jest a-standin' here in this cold!" declared Susannah. "Let's shuck corn!"

When we'd hauled the corn in baskets to the barn and dumped it in a heap, we all settled down to the task of ripping off the husks. Once we set to work, we warmed up some, what with the barn animals' steamy breath around us and being sheltered from the wind.

Susannah hopped around the barn like a crow in her black dress and cape, stripping the corn with quick, sharp fingers, her elbows flapping at her sides. She collected the fallen husks to dry for stuffing bed ticks the way a crow hunts up shreds of cornstalk to line its nest.

Henry sat on a stool with three barrels behind him, and we set the baskets of stripped ears at his feet.

"Now here's a fine ear of corn!" he admired, holding one up and running his finger along the smooth, yellow kernels. "This'll make us nice, sweet corn pone in the winter." He tossed it into the barrel meant for our winter's provisions, then picked up another. Picking off the silky threads that clung to it, he held it up for a good close look, turning it this way and that. "Now, this one here, this ain't quite as nice," he said. "This'll feed Sally and Lazarus." He threw it into the second barrel, then pointed a finger at a little pile of spoiled corn I'd set to the side of me. "Don't cast that aside, boy! The cow and the hogs gotta eat too, and that corn there is plenty good for them." I gathered up the pile and pushed it his way so he could throw it in the third barrel.

Maggie'd spread a worn-out quilt on the barn floor near Henry's feet, and there Jimmy lay, rolling from his back to his tummy over and over again. Now and then Henry got off his stool and set his grandson back in the blanket's middle, feeling the child's ears to satisfy himself that they weren't too cold. Sometimes the old man stopped working, cracked his knuckles, picked up his fiddle, and scratched us out a song or two. He tapped his toe, singing,

> *Oh I'm a-goin' to the shuckin'!*
> *I'm a-goin' to the shuckin' of the corn....*

Mountain tunes, he called them—songs he'd learned as a boy back in east Tennessee. That was before he left his father's worn-out tobacco farm and struck out alone for Missouri. He was barely grown-up then, just eighteen years old, but he rode a pack mule all the way to Pittsburgh. That's where he hewed out some timber and built himself a flatboat. Leaving the mule behind, he floated down the Ohio River to St. Louis, then he walked all the way to Locust Creek country, just him and his old flintlock rifle.

"I spent my first winter here sleeping in a hollow sycamore log," he told us as he pitched a steady stream of corn behind him into the barrels. "I had the ague something awful! I lay a-shiverin' in that log, wrapped up in a thin blanket, gettin' ready to meet my Maker."

I left off husking and stared up at the old man, open-mouthed. He winked an eye when he looked down at me, but kept right on working.

"Fox Indians came and mixed me up some medicine yarbs." He smiled. "Yes, they was good folk. Kept me alive that winter. Taught me how to bury corn in sacks made of bark to keep it good till the next harvest. It's a smart settler, Jacob, who learns the ways of the Indians!"

Eliza cocked her head and squinted up at Henry, her nose twitching like it did whenever she was getting ready to pester someone with one of her questions. After a second or two of scaring up her courage, she came out with it. "What's a squaw man?"

Old Henry didn't bat an eye. "You mean that what's painted on my store? That's me. I'm the squaw man."

Eliza giggled. "A squaw's an Indian lady."

"Sometimes. And it's what white folks used to sometimes call men like me on account of I lived with the Indians, and took their ways as my own."

Eliza giggled again.

"Go on, laugh! They meant it as a shame to me, but I wear the name proud. Back when I first showed up in Missouri, most white folk thought the only good Indian was a dead one. But me...I became blood brother to the Fox tribe—the Red Earth People. I trapped, hunted, and traded with both whites and Indians till I built me up a trading post. That's my store. Course, now I get paid money for my goods. Back then, no one paid. Just swapped me honey, grain, or tools. Anything ye can think of, I swapped for."

"Why are you called Captain?" I asked, going back to my shucking.

A fiery shine came into the old man's eyes. "Because all that ain't to say I weren't loyal to Uncle Sam." He spat on the barn floor in disgust. "I'm called Captain because of the Sauk. The Yellow Earth People." He squeezed his eyes shut tight, remembering. "Nigh thirty years ago now, Old Black Hawk of the Sauks kicked up such a fuss up in Illinois that Governor Miller called up volunteers to go out and meet him. I joined the militia and they made me a Captain right off. Well, the Sauk never did come down into Missouri, and most of the volunteers came back. But I had no family then, and no reason to hurry home. I stayed on till Blackhawk was captured the next year. Looky here!"

Henry bent over and rubbed his palm along the center of his scalp, over the rough skin and a few straggling hairs. "A Sauk warrior scalped me!" He pointed to two round white scars on the crown of his head. "Army doctor pegged my skull. Drilled holes right into it, till bloody water oozed out. It didn't take but two years for the skin to grow back." Patting his head in a satisfied way, he straightened up again. "Old Blackhawk and his Sauks put up a good fight, yes sir!" he hooted, slapping his knee with an ear of corn. "But he couldn't beat Uncle Sam." Henry rubbed his stubbly chin and looked at the floor awhile. When he spoke again his voice was soft. "The Fox tribe moved out West soon after I came home, and I was right sorry to see 'em go."

"That how your leg got hurt too? Fightin' Sauks?" Eliza asked.

"Arrow split my shin," he replied, rubbing the old wound. "That time I couldn't get no doctor's help, 'cause we were stuck in the woods. Another militia man soaked my wound, put moss on it, and wrapped it up in elm bark. It healed up all right, but it never did feel quite the same after that."

Eliza, who'd left off working when Henry began to talk, sat twisting one of her braids around her finger.

"Idle hands are a young girl's undoin'!" scolded Susannah, stomping across the barn on her wooden heels, hands on hips. Eliza got that pouty look she always wore when she didn't want to do her share of the work, but after one eyeful of that fierce old woman she wiped it off quick. Her hands got busy enough then, but Susannah kept her eye on Eliza just the same. She came closer. Kneeling down, she took Eliza's chin into her gnarled old hand and turned her face this way and that, studying it.

"Freckles!" she muttered. "Now listen here, girl. Come spring, ye collect some dew off a spider's web, and wash yer face in it. Those freckles will disappear, like as not!"

Maggie looked up from her shucking. "I expect wearin' a sunbonnet will do the same, Ma."

Susannah let go of Eliza's face and swiped a hand Maggie's way as if to shoo away her doubts. "Ye just see if it don't help!" she snapped, hopping back across the barn to attend to her work.

That night we returned to the house cold and tired, but mighty pleased with our little harvest. Maggie brought a dried berry pie out of the cellar and boiled us up a succotash to celebrate the shucking. I'd always been partial to that stew of beans, corn, and salt pork, and as I sat shoveling it in Henry jabbed me in the ribs with his elbow.

"This here stew tasted a whole lot better with bear's flesh in it. But I ain't eaten it that way for over thirty years now." He shook his head sadly, then spooned another heap up into his mouth.

Sitting around the fire that night, I felt a mighty satisfaction in knowing I'd helped to earn my keep. I'd shucked my hands raw, but we'd laid by enough corn for the winter, and even had some left over to sell. I lay on the rag hearth rug with my head in my hands, looking up at the ceiling. Strings of dried apples and pumpkin rings stretched from one wall to another. A bowl heaped up with nuts sat on the hearth for the taking; I heard Eliza cracking them beside me and smelled the shells burning in the fire.

Were my folks as well provided for as Eliza and me? Did they have a roof over their heads, and provisions in a barn? Had some merciful soul taken them in until they could find a place of their own? Or were they wandering like the folk in the wagons we'd seen rolling east, looking for shelter, hungry and cold? Jerusha and Sarah were so little, and winter was coming on fast. I could see them now, my sisters' fat little faces all chapped and red from the wind. I heard Sarah cry out then, a sharp cry that pierced my brain and tore at my heart. I sat up quick and rubbed my eyes. I'd drifted to sleep in the warmth of the fire, and had heard Jimmy squeal on his grandmammy's lap as she cuddled him in the rocker.

"Hush, hush, boy," she murmured, lifting him to her shoulder and rocking faster.

"I declare," sighed Maggie, "but it's good to be done with the shucking. It's a happy day. Give us a song, Pa!"

Henry obliged, bending over his fiddle and scratching out reels and jigs till his arm tired out. Then he stopped fiddling, tapped his toe, and sang,

> *Shady Grove, my true love,*
> *Shady Grove, I say,*
> *Shady Grove, my true love,*
> *I'm a-goin' away.*
>
> *Peaches in the springtime,*
> *Apples in the fall;*
> *If I can't have my own true love,*
> *I'll have no love at all.*

I tapped my toe to the music, cracking and eating nuts till I was near to bursting. When the old man started in on a lullaby for his grandbaby, I lay back again on the rug, feeling sleepy myself. I hadn't lain there long when Susannah let out a shriek that jerked me upright.

"Jacob! Fetch me the axe. Be quick, boy!" I jumped to my feet and ran like the Devil himself out the kitchen door to the woodpile, grabbing up the axe and running back to where the old woman sat with the baby on her lap. She motioned to Henry to take the axe, which he did, while I stood trying to catch my breath, waiting to see what for. Henry leaned over the baby. Gently, between thumb and forefinger, he picked a wood tick off Jimmy's fat little wrist, and slew it by pushing it into the axe blade.

"There now!" Susannah nodded with a satisfied grin. "We've killed the child's first tick on a tool! This boy'll grow up to be a fine workman, ye all mark my words!"

Maggie tossed aside her mending and jumped up from her seat. She stomped over to her pa and grabbed the axe from his hand, throwing it down on the hearth with a clattering thud. "I declare, you two carry on like you're still in the Tennessee hills, while we're livin' in a day of telegraphs and trains. Shoot, Ma, before long I might even have me a real cookstove, 'stead of cooking over the fire." She shook her head. "I may be poor, but I ain't superstitious!"

Henry shook his head. "Send a girl to school, and what do ye get? I knowed ye ought to have stayed at home those six years. We're proud to be mountain folk, Maggie, but now ye're ashamed on us!"

Maggie looked sorry. "No, Pa. I ain't ashamed. But just look at yourself, dressed in buckskin like back in Indian days, with that old tomahawk hangin' from your belt." She lifted Jimmy off Susannah's lap and returned to her chair.

"I wear a suit of a Sunday!"

"I know, Pa. I was just sayin'."

Henry stood staring at his boots, his shoulders sagging, one hand resting on the handle of his tomahawk. "I reckon a man dresses his whole life like he did when he was happiest," he murmured before stooping to pick up his fiddle.

Susannah pulled her pipe out of her apron pocket and lit it behind a cupped hand, drawing a deep draught of the sweet heavy smoke. "Bah! Young folk today!" she scoffed, then set to puffing away contentedly as she rocked before the fire. Henry tuned his fiddle once again and made it whine out a slow, sad song. As I listened with my eyes closed I could almost see his pa's tobacco farm in the Tennessee hills, and Henry the boy running barefoot in the summer, just like me. Then he tapped his foot faster, calling to his wife as he fiddled up a fury, "Do a clog, Susannah! Do a clog!"

And gray-haired Susannah in her long black dress, her pipe still in her teeth, stood up, lifted up her skirts, and began to rock and kick and stomp on her wooden heels before the fire. Eliza and I scooted out of her way, clapping our hands in time to her feet, while Maggie bounced Jimmy on her knee. Susannah danced until the fire began to die, her heels pounding the floorboards, echoing through all the dark corners of the house.

Early next morning I went out to the barn to hitch Lazarus up to the wagon.

"Come on, Lazarus. Get up!" I ordered. That mule lay on the floor of the barn and looked up at me like he thought he was General Price himself. In fact, I had no doubt he'd run off and join himself up with the Confederate army if mules could do such things. "You old Rebel mule!" I shouted at him. He rolled his eyes and let out a screechy snort, not making a move. Disgusted, I lifted up both my hands like I imagined Jesus did, and yelled, "Lazarus! Come forth!" He just stared up at me, looking confused, and I laughed to myself, thinking maybe that's how all the people looked at Jesus too. Well, not having the powers of the Savior himself, I had to slap, pull, kick, and wrestle that mule to his feet, with him fussing and complaining in my ear the whole time.

When I finally got him hitched to the wagon, Eliza was already up in the seat, bundled up against the wind and holding Jimmy in her lap. Together Maggie and I heaved four fat, wriggling hogs into the wagon box, along with two big sacks of corn. Then we took off toward Linneus.

The wind flattened the grass on the unplowed hills and cut through the hollows like a knife. A light, drizzling rain pricked our faces, wetting our wraps and glistening on the hogs' backs. Swaying to and fro on the wagon seat, I watched the unfamiliar countryside roll past: fields of dead cornstalks, naked hills, thick clumps of oaks lifting black, wet twig arms to the sky. Cottontails scattered from the roadside brush as we creaked by, darting up into the fields and woods. A deer on the brow of a hill stood still as a stump, watching us pass, twitching his snow-white tail.

The wagon rattled uphill and down, and we were no more than a half mile from Linneus when something big and black loomed up on our right. Straight up out of a hillside jutted the charred skeleton of a house, half of it collapsed in on itself and the other half still standing. A lone buzzard hawk perched on the scorched chimney.

Just laying eyes on that burnt-up carcass of a building gave me a wrenching in my gut. I turned and peeked over Eliza's head at Maggie, but she was staring straight ahead, cracking the whip for Lazarus to move on faster.

Eliza gaped at the ruin with a sad, pale face, then burst out with the question I myself could hardly keep down. "What happened there?"

Maggie whipped Lazarus on a second time and kept her face turned forward like she hadn't heard.

Straight up out of a hillside jutted the charred skeleton of a house, half of it collapsed in on itself.

"What burnt down, Maggie?" she hollered louder, over the wind and the rattling of the wheels. All of a sudden Maggie jerked hard on the reins and halted the wagon right there in the road. When she turned to us I saw all the light had gone out of her eyes.

"Clem burnt it down," she sighed. "It was Asa Wheeler's house. Burnt down the barn too, stole his horse, then he run off. That was in July. We ain't seen him since."

I swallowed hard. "Why'd he do it?"

"No one knows, Jacob. Oh, Clem and Asa had their differences all right, but nothin' big enough to bring this on. One day Clem told me he was headed over to the Wheeler place. He didn't come home for three days. When he finally did show up, he wasn't himself. He seemed nervous and jittery, always lookin' over his shoulder. When I asked him what was wrong, all he'd say was that he'd taken the oath and I shouldn't worry. Well, I'd always known Clem was a Union man, like my pa. But two days later he did this." Maggie cleared her throat and stared at the charred house. "Then he was gone. Now I hear tell he's a Rebel, and I just can't figure why."

I sat quiet a minute, getting up courage enough to ask Maggie the one question that'd been on my mind since the day I'd learned she was married to a Rebel. "Maggie, are you Secesh?"

"Me?" she said, clucking to the mule till the wagon lurched forward. "Womenfolk go along with their husbands in these things, generally. Clem and I were always Union folk, just like Ma and Pa. When Clem burnt down that house and run off, I felt confused inside. I couldn't all of a sudden reckon myself a Rebel! But Clem's still my husband. Yessir, I'm confused, like

Missouri. I'm as torn up inside as this state, and I don't rightly know what side I belong on anymore. I guess I'm just tryin' to outlive this war, Jacob, and the end of it can't come soon enough for me."

We rolled on in silence then. But half turned around in my seat, I watched the black skeleton grow smaller and smaller until it finally disappeared in the mist behind us.

The Agreement

M y land!" exclaimed Maggie as we rolled into town. "Look at them all!"

A swarm of Union soldiers had settled at the town's edge, camped as thick as ants on a fallen plum. They stood around their tents in shiny-buttoned blue, looking just like I'd imagined they would, tall and fine, with trimmed mustaches and pistols on their belts. Some walked through the streets in twos, or leaned against the door frames of shops, smoking cigars and watching the ladies walk past. Others huddled around fires, warming their hands, now and then shooting a sharp burst of laughter like gunfire into the thick white mist.

A banner stretched across the opening of the biggest tent invited all comers between ages eighteen and thirty-five to join up and fight for the Union. "Six months! One year! Two years! Earn twelve dollars a month!" called out a soldier as we passed. When he looked up and saw no grown man in our wagon, he smiled and waved us on. If I'd even been close to eighteen years old that day I'd have fairly flown off that wagon seat. How I ached to join those Yankees. Dressed and armed and sent out by Uncle Sam, they drew pay for doing what I dreamed of doing night and day: whipping the pants off the Rebels.

A strong satisfaction came over me in the middle of all those Federals, and I felt safer than I had in a long time. Another sign, strung up on a tent pole with wire, told us this was an Illinois regiment. I knew they'd come down to grab hold of Missouri before she slipped south, to latch on to her tight and keep her in the Union. I was glad they were here. Now I could rest some, let down my guard a little, knowing the Federal army was close at hand.

Maggie yanked Lazarus to a halt in front of one of the big tents and asked to speak to an officer. One came out right away, hoisting up his britches, a fat cigar dangling from his lips.

"Ma'am?"

"Beg pardon, sir. But will you buy four hogs and two sacks of corn for your men?"

The large-bellied man strolled up close to the wagon box and gave the hogs a good looking over. He opened one of the sacks and rolled some of the yellow kernels around in his palm. Then he pulled out his leather pocketbook and gave Maggie just about twice what those hogs and the corn were worth. She didn't blink an eye. When he called over some of his men to unload the provisions, Maggie leaned close to my ear.

"Pa said they'd pay good money for food," she whispered, "with all the mouths they've got to feed. Now we can order you boots, Jacob!" I looked down at Clem's old work boots I'd been shuffling around in, and smiled to think I'd get them off my feet before long.

"Jacob, look!" Eliza shook my arm when we circled around the Yankee tents to enter town on High Street. Stuck onto the Union camp like a spider's web and sprawled out into the fields at town's edge was a shantytown made of crude shelters. A whole mess of folks had thrown up whatever they could find:

scrap boards, canvas wagon covers, sticks, branches, or thin-worn army tents no longer fit for soldiers to use. Grannies hushed crying babies as they sat huddled beneath wagon boxes. Women washed and cooked, the smoke from their fires curling like thin gray ribbons into the sky. A skinny, brown-haired girl in a ripped blue apron stood sucking her fingers and hugging a doll as she watched us pass by. When our wagon drew up close to her I could see that the doll was just an old boot. Someone had carved a face into the heel and tied twig arms onto the middle with twine, then dressed it up by wrapping a faded handkerchief around it.

A puny boy poked his dirty face out of a tent opening. He burst out to join five more just like him as they chased our wagon, whipping our wheels with willow branches and yelling "Haw!" like they'd heard grown-ups do.

"Poor souls." Maggie shook her head and flapped the reins to move us along quicker.

"Who are they?" asked Eliza, scooting closer to Maggie and slipping an arm through hers.

"Folks driven out by the Rebels, I reckon. Come to the Yankees for protection." As Maggie drove on past the courthouse toward some shops farther down High Street, Eliza caught my eye. I knew she was thinking the same as me. If our folks weren't in Iowa right now, could they be in a shantytown like this one?

A man walking down the courthouse steps stopped when he saw us coming. He was small and fidgety, half swallowed up in a coat two sizes too big for him. After giving him a quick glance, Maggie set her face to the road ahead and cracked the whip. Staring hard at Maggie through narrowed eyes, he folded his arms across his chest and turned his whole body along with us as we passed him by. When I twisted in my seat to gape back at him, he screwed up his lips and spit in our direction. Then he stomped off the opposite way. When I looked back at Maggie's face, I saw she'd set her mouth in the hard, straight line she wore when she didn't welcome questions.

Maggie pulled to a stop in front of a small store called Metzger's Boots and Shoes. She jumped down and took Jimmy from Eliza, nodding toward the shop to let me know that was where we'd do our buying.

"I'm gonna get new boots!" I told Lazarus as I tethered him to a post and opened up a small feed sack. He hiked up his tail and let loose in the rear, dropping a load that landed with a mighty thud in the street. "Aw, go on and eat," I said, holding the shelled corn right under his nose. When he'd finished it off, I followed Maggie and Eliza into the store.

"One minute, please!" called a woman's voice from a back room. Out stepped a fancy-dressed lady with a smile on her face, but the smile became a smirk when she set eyes on Maggie. Folding her arms, she pinched her lips together like she'd just bit into a sour apple. "Mrs. Canaday," she said.

"Mrs. Metzger," replied Maggie, gone all red in the face.

The woman didn't speak again, just looked from Maggie to me, then to Eliza holding little Jimmy. She waited.

"We're in need of boots today," Maggie said.

The woman looked us over a second time. "Would these be your kinfolk, Mrs. Canaday?"

"No," answered Maggie. "Jacob and Eliza are passin' through, bound for Iowa. They intend to bide with me this winter."

"Children, alone?"

Maggie opened her mouth and closed it again. She nodded.

"Refugees?" Mrs. Metzger raised her eyebrows. "Well, I'd be surprised if you could provide for them, Mrs. Canaday. What with your husband and all—"

"We'll do fine, Mrs. Metzger," snapped Maggie, turning away and grabbing up a fancy lady's shoe to inspect. The boot maker's wife turned on her heels and strutted into the back room. She soon marched back in with her husband.

Metzger was a short, round man in a leather apron. Fat, sausage arms all covered with red, curly hair stuck out of his rolled-up sleeves. While his wife stood behind him with her chin in the air, he flashed a big smile and came right toward me with a hand out.

"Well, well!" he exclaimed, shaking my arm and nodding his head. "Mrs. Canaday wants boots today, ja? Sit right down."

I sat down and stuck my feet out toward him.

"You children must be new in Linneus," he guessed as he knelt down to measure my feet. "I never did see you before this, I think."

"Yes sir," I replied.

"They're refugees, Johann," put in Mrs. Metzger from across the room.

He raised his eyebrows. "Ja? Ach, I am sorry to hear it."

I looked up at Maggie. "We're gettin' by," I told him.

"Jacob and Eliza know how to earn their keep," added Maggie.

"Sure, sure." The boot maker nodded, scribbling my measurements down on an old scrap of leather. "Ja, we Germans love the Union, Jacob. I am not born in this country, but I come to St. Louis when just a little boy. I hurt to see what all happens in Missouri nowadays! I got three brothers in the Union army.

Me, I wanted to join up, but I'm not young like them no more. Instead, I sell boots to soldiers. Cheap, of course!" He roared out a laugh as he struggled to his feet. He walked us to the door and shook my hand, then took Maggie's hand in his and bowed like a gentleman. "I thank you much, Mrs. Canaday." He smiled and opened the door for us to go out. "In two weeks, your boots will be finished. I have much work these days."

As we walked into the street my eyes wandered back toward the refugee camp at the edge of town. I stopped. From where I stood I could see the smoke from its fires drifting up through the drizzling rain. There must have been at least a hundred and fifty families in that tangled mess of wanderers. Could my folks be among them?

"Jacob?" Maggie said softly, putting a hand on my shoulder. She followed the direction of my eyes and then she knew. "Go and look, Jacob. I'll be about my errands." She lifted Jimmy out of Eliza's arms. "Go with your brother," Maggie said to her.

I grabbed Eliza's hand and led her toward the refugee camp. Winding our way through it, we peeked inside tents, under wagons, and studied the faces around each cooking fire. We asked everyone who'd listen if they'd seen or heard of our folks, but no one had. In all that crowd there was hardly a man to be seen, except for white-headed grandpas. We saw mostly women, frying up corn fritters for their little ones, scrubbing clothes in barrels, going about their everyday chores while crouching behind the Federal army for protection. We'd looked through nearly the whole camp when Eliza stopped and yanked on my sleeve.

"Jacob!" she said. "Listen."

A woman was talking somewhere to our left. Between the rattle of pots and pans and crying babies I could hear her speak the name "Sarah" two or three times. Ma! Scrambling right over someone's bedroll, I pushed my way toward that voice.

"Where's Sarah?" I called out. "Who said that name?" An old man sitting by a fire pointed toward a woman in a woolen shawl and black skirt. She stood with her back to me, bent over a wooden tub, washing a small child.

"Ma?" I stumbled toward her, nearly tripping over a wadded-up wagon canvas and two grain sacks. "Ma!" Reaching out my hand, I grabbed a fistful of her shawl and pulled. It slipped off her shoulders and she wheeled around to snatch it back. Her baby squealed and splashed, laughing in the tub. Water sprayed everywhere.

I dropped my chin to my chest. "I'm sorry, ma'am. I just...I...."

Her face softened. "It's all right, son."

Half blinded by tears, I backed away from her.

"God bless you, boy," she said, her voice full of pity.

I bolted back to Eliza and grabbed her by the arm. "They ain't here," I said. "Let's go."

Maggie stood waiting for us by the mule, watching us walk toward her with our heads hanging down. "I want to tell you something," she said when we drew up close. "I married late. All I ever wanted was a house full of laughin' children. I'm pleased you all came to my door, and I'm proud to give you shelter. You've cut my loneliness clean in two!" She took Eliza by the hand, saying, "Come, girl, and show me which cloth you admire. I mean to sew you a Sunday dress just as quick as I can, and your brother needs a coat." She started off toward the millinery.

I'd just set out to follow her when a door banged shut behind me. I wheeled around and saw the boot maker strolling out onto the walk, his hands deep in his leather apron pockets.

"Come inside, Jacob, out of the cold," he offered.

I looked across the street. Maggie and Eliza had disappeared into the millinery. "I'd be grateful," I replied, glad not to have to look at endless bolts of cloth.

His shop was empty. I sat myself down on a chair, brushing the drizzle off my coat. Metzger turned the key in the door and flipped around a sign hanging from a nail above the window so the side facing me said Open. He smiled and drew a chair up close beside mine. He spun it around and straddled it, crossing his hairy arms on its back and looking straight into my face.

Out the corner of my eye I saw a figure slide out from the back room. Glancing over, I expected to see Mrs. Metzger, but instead I saw the man from the courthouse steps, the one who'd spit after us. Metzger stuck out the toe of his shoe and hooked the leg of a nearby stool. He pulled it close, waving the man over. The spitter shuffled across the floorboards, running a nervous hand through his uncombed hair. His eyes locked onto mine as he sat down, making me squirm in my seat and wish I'd stayed outside. But Metzger laughed and clapped the man on his back, putting me more at ease.

"Jacob," he said, smiling, "here is my friend, Asa Wheeler. Asa, here is Jacob..."

"Knight," I said.

Asa reached a hand my way. Remembering the sight of him spitting at us, I hesitated a second. Then I stuck mine out and gave his a short shake. His hand was cold and grasping, and a shiver ran up my arm and neck.

Metzger cleared his throat and scooted his chair an inch or two closer to mine. He drew Asa in, patting him on the back. "Now you speak with the boy."

Asa nodded, then let loose a spray of words like buckshot. "What I have to say I'll say simple and quick. I'll wager you're a refugee from down south, or out west. That so, Jacob?"

I had nothing to hide, so I nodded.

"Run off your land by Rebels?"

"Yes sir."

Asa shot the boot maker a satisfied smile. "That's hard luck, son. And your folks?" I opened my mouth, but shut it again. No words would come.

"Dead?"

"No!" I cried. "I mean...well, Ma told me to run, and when we went home...they were gone."

"They never came back for you?"

I hung my head. "No sir."

Asa patted my shoulder with a few short, jerking thumps. "We've all got hurt by this war, son. Missouri's bleeding bad. Well, listen up good, boy. Most of us in this town are Union folk. But I wonder if you know you're living under a Rebel's roof? Mrs. Canaday's husband is a known bushwhacker, wanted by the Union army for oath-breaking and taking up arms against the Union."

"Can it be you saw that burnt-up house just west of town, Jacob?" asked Metzger.

I nodded.

"Well, that was my house," declared Asa, the muscles in his jaw drawing tight. "Clem Canaday torched it one night, then run off. Torched it because he knew I'm a Union man! Stole my one good horse, too. Now my family's got to live with kinfolk here in town, begging charity to get by."

His words sank into my gut like a rock. I wanted to tell him I'd seen his burnt-up home...that my home lay in a heap of ashes too, but the best I could do was swallow hard and nod my head.

"We want no Rebels in this town, Jacob," continued Metzger. "I see you are a good boy, so I tell you—"

"Clem Canaday's joined himself up with a band of bush-whackers!" butted in Asa. "He ain't nothing but a pain in the Federal army's rear end! He's been blowing up bridges and burning down barns, and God knows what all else!"

My breath came fast and hot blood rose into my face. Somewhere deep inside myself I heard Ma screaming, saw little Sarah's eyes grow wide with terror.

Asa's voice dropped to a whisper. "Bushwhackers like Clem got to be brought down, Jacob. Now, there's a group of us in this town wanting to see justice done. Call ourselves the Vigilance Committee. If Clem Canaday thinks he can hide out on his farm till his deeds blow over, we aim to prove him wrong. Vengeance is my right, Jacob. I'm going to be the one to hang him!"

Metzger placed a fat hand on the angry man's shoulder to quiet him. "You see, Jacob, the law says if Mrs. Canaday takes her husband in she is no better than a bushwhacker herself. She would be guilty, along with her husband, of breaking the oath."

"The Yankees'll seize her property if she's found guilty of that," added Asa. "Son, it'd be a protection to her if you turned Clem in to us when he returns."

As he spoke I closed my eyes. I felt myself racing through the corn, the leaf blades cutting into my face. Spinning around in the field I saw flames shooting up from the barn, heard again the squeal of the hogs running loose, the report of a rifle.

"And what if he don't?" I whispered, opening my eyes.

The two men looked at each other and smiled. "Winter's coming on quick, Jacob," said Asa. "The cold'll drive him home, sure enough. He'll want food, warm clothes. He'll want to see his wife and baby."

"And I will make it worth your trouble, boy," added the boot maker, setting a hand on my knee, patting it kindly. He tilted his head toward the money box on the counter. "You just come to me if you see that bushwhacker, ja?"

I stared at the floor, thinking on what Maggie had just said about how we'd cut her loneliness in two. Because of her, my sister was well again and my feet were healed. We had plenty to eat and a warm bed to sleep in. Maggie was so kind; it made me sick to think how her husband had turned outlaw. She was loyal to him, that much I knew—too loyal for her own good. Maybe if I turned him in, I'd be protecting her.

I looked up at Metzger and Asa Wheeler. They sat silent, staring at me, waiting. I rubbed my face with my hands and lowered my forehead onto my knuckles. Something felt cracked inside me. Loud and clear I heard Pa's wild scream echoing across the cornfield. Those bushwhackers had shot him. Had I been fooling myself, thinking he'd fought them off and escaped to Iowa?

Slowly I raised my head. I knew I ought to speak, but there was nothing to say. I nodded to show them both that I could be counted on.

Asa Wheeler jumped up from his seat, eagerly rubbing his hands together. "It'll do us both good, boy, to see justice done. The sooner the better!"

"All in good time, Asa." Metzger smiled and laid an arm across my shoulders. He led me to the door. "All in good time. I wait for you here then, Jacob."

Maggie and Eliza were just coming out of the millinery. When we'd loaded up our store-bought goods, we untied Lazarus and headed back toward the square. There, something nailed to the courthouse wall caught my eye. As we drew closer I could see it was a wanted poster, soaked with rain and flapping in the wind. In between gusts I saw clearly the name CANADAY. My chest went tight; I sneaked a glance at Maggie. She'd seen it too, slowing down the mule to get a good look. Silently she stared, her hands gone so limp the reins slipped right out.

"Maggie?" Eliza, holding Jimmy, reached over and nudged her. "Maggie, Jimmy's gettin' cold."

Startled, Maggie shook her head, then cracked the whip so hard the wagon lurched forward, nearly pitching me off the seat. Before we crossed the square to head out of town, I looked over my shoulder. Metzger stood leaning against the door of his shop, his arms folded across his chest. Outside on the walk, bareheaded in the rain, stood Asa Wheeler, watching us go.

War
Hatchet

Winter blew down from the north, driving biting snowflakes in front of it. Eliza and I crawled into bed each night and pressed our backs together to stay warm. One night Eliza whispered, "Do you think Ma and Pa and Jerusha and Sarah are keepin' warm now, Jacob?"

I lay quiet a minute. "Course they are," I whispered back.

"Those refugees near Linneus," she went on, "we might've been like them if Maggie hadn't taken us in."

"That's true enough," I replied. Just when I thought she must have fallen asleep I heard her sniffling. "What is it?" I asked.

"Jacob, I can't stop wonderin'…why didn't Ma and Pa come back for us? Didn't they know we'd hurry back to the house next mornin'?"

"Now, Eliza," I sighed. "You know they would've come if they could. They just figured I'd be more than able to get you and me on up to Iowa without their help. Why, they're waitin' for us there right now. When spring comes, we'll join 'em."

Eliza sniffled awhile. When I finally heard her breath turn slow and heavy, I felt relieved. Lying beside her, I hoped with all my might she'd believed my words. I needed her to believe, since I wasn't so sure I could anymore.

The chill November air seeped through the attic walls, making it hard to get up and dressed at chore time. But hog killing day was always a pleasure to see, and I was already buttoning up my shirt when Maggie's rooster crowed for the first time that morning.

"Wake up, it's hog killin' day!" I shook Eliza and pulled on my new boots. Through the frost on the window I could see Henry and Susannah trudging up the drive through deep snow, hauling a big iron cauldron between them. Henry's dogs trotted close at his heels, for Henry never went anywhere without them.

Back home before the war started, all our neighbors came to help us kill our hogs. We'd scald, scrape, cut, and salt the meat most of the day, then cook up a big feast that night to celebrate. Pulling on my clothes, I could almost taste the tender ribs we used to gnaw on late into the night as we sat around the fire.

Today the five of us were enough to do the job. Maggie only had three hogs to kill, leaving one male and one female to make next year's crop. Just as soon as we'd downed a breakfast of corn mush and biscuits, we set to work. Henry and I butchered the hogs outside, then scalded them in Susannah's big pot. We chopped them up with axes and put the meat in a hollowed log trough to take salt. Then I carried the stinking hogs' bowels into the kitchen and began to clean them, while Maggie and Susannah pounded fatty scraps of meat to mush for stuffing inside the casings.

Eliza kept wandering away, hanging around the kitchen door, wasting good fat scraps by tossing them to Calhoun and Henry's dogs. Finally Susannah took hold of her ear with a bloody, greasy hand and pulled her back to the chopping block.

"It stinks in this kitchen!" whined Eliza. "My stomach goes all sick at hog-killin' time."

Susannah pounded hard on the block. "Would ye rather sniff daisies or have bacon to eat this winter, child?"

Eliza sighed, sagging her shoulders. "Ma never made me clean hog bowels or pound scraps. She let me roast the hogs' ears outside."

"I declare, ye know next to nothin' about providin' for a family," Susannah chided, shaking her head and clucking. "Will ye be a spinster all yer life? What man'll marry a lazy good-for-nothin', that's what I'd like to know?"

"Now, as I recall," put in Henry, bent over the meat trough just outside the kitchen door, "Susannah herself could barely stand the sight or smell of a hog killin' at the time I married her!"

The old woman spun around, her mouth drawn tight. "And what if I was more refined than ye? Back in Virginny we had slaves to do our butcherin'." She set to pounding again, then stopped. "Lordy, it's been nigh thirty-five years ago I left there. This hard life runs fast like a river!"

"Ma, tell the children about when you first met Pa," begged Maggie, laughing.

"Bah!"

"Yes, Ma, tell it."

Susannah whacked her mallet hard on the block and turned toward her husband. She waved the bloody mallet at him just like a high and mighty judge, but a smile was on her face. "The day I first laid eyes on Henry Wilkinson he was dressed like an Injun in nothin' but a breech clout and doeskin leggin's with his naked back end all hangin' out! He had that tommyhawk danglin' from his belt and I thought, 'Lord have mercy, it's a white savage!' My ma tried to shield my eyes from the indecency of it all, on account of we were proper folk, not accustomed to such crude sights."

As I bent my head to hide a smile, I heard Maggie and Eliza laughing.

Henry straightened himself up and stepped over the kitchen threshold. "But it didn't take ye long to decide to marry me, now did it?"

"No, Henry," she replied, grabbing up a clean hog's bowel and shoving the meat mush inside. "Yer cabin was a heap farther along than my pa's and it had a bigger fireplace in it." She stuffed the sausage near to bursting. When she spoke again her voice was low and faraway sounding. "Then came little John, William, Henry Junior, and Joel."

"Boys?" I asked, surprised. I hadn't thought of Maggie having brothers. "Where are they?"

"Scattered all over these hills, child." Susannah twisted a knot in the end of her sausage, a little sadness creeping into her voice. "They grew up wild, what with no kinfolk to help guide 'em. My ma and pa lit out for Oregon in the forties, and we was left all alone here."

Henry hoisted up his britches and stuck out his chest. "My boys are independent, just like I raised 'em to be. No son of mine clings to his mama's apron strings. Besides, Joel ain't far...just over in Linneus."

"You'd think he was out in Oregon for all we see him. Well, I thank God I've got Margaret," Susannah told him, looking him in the eye. "It's a comfort to a poor woman's heart to have a daughter late in life. I pray she never goes. I couldn't bear to part from kinfolk again, the way I had to when my pa dragged us all out here from Virginny."

Henry guffawed. "Shoot, woman, it's a better life out here than in Virginny! That's why yer pa asked ye all to come out here so long ago."

Susannah picked up her mallet and slammed it down on the block with an ear-splitting crack. Gazing beyond Henry and out the window, she said softly to herself, "He never asked."

~

As Christmas drew near, Maggie pulled Eliza into the kitchen each day and made her bake sweetbreads and pies to go down cellar. Then one day she showed her how to mix up a molasses cake with white sugar sprinkled on top of it. Bringing in wood for the fire, I stopped and looked over Eliza's shoulder, taking in the rich, warm smell of the molasses.

"Can't wait to eat a slice of that one," I said.

"I can," she replied. "I'm so sick of bakin' I don't want to see another cake till next Christmas."

"Why, you lazy whiner!" I grabbed hold of one of her braids and flicked it in her face. "You want Maggie to serve you hand and foot?" I walked away, disgusted with my sister, but pleased with the sweet, spicy smells in the house. Ma had always baked molasses cake at Christmastime. Smelling it made me feel like she was near.

On Christmas morning, a squawking flurry in the henhouse woke me long before sunup. A door banged below, and Jimmy let out a wail from his bed across the hall in Maggie's room. I shot up in bed. Who'd slammed the door? Had Clem come home for Christmas? Hurrying over the cold floor in my bare feet, I scooped Jimmy up in my arms and carried him below, looking for his ma.

Maggie came in the kitchen door just as I reached the last step, her shotgun in one hand, her hair shiny wet with melting snow. She'd been out in her nightdress and bare feet.

"What is it?" I asked, holding tight to Jimmy, who squirmed and squealed at the sight of her.

She lay the gun on the kitchen table and grabbed up a dish-cloth to wipe her hair dry. "Fox, I reckon. Don't let it trouble you, Jacob. Go on back upstairs."

"Fox!" I cried. "How many chickens did he kill?"

Maggie looked dizzy. She slung the dishcloth over the back of a chair and leaned on it for support. "Just one's all."

"Just one? Couldn't be no fox!" I crossed the room and set Jimmy down on the hearth rug. Then I grabbed up her gun and started for the door, but Maggie caught my arm and pulled the gun away. "There's bound to be tracks!" I blurted out.

"Leave it be, Jacob. It's done."

"What's the matter with Calhoun, anyhow? He didn't even make a sound."

"Gettin' old, I reckon," she replied. "Well, go on back to bed, Jacob. We all deserve a rest on Christmas day." She waved me back toward the stairs, smiling, but beneath the smile I could see her lips trembling.

Back in the attic, I opened my window and leaned out as far as I could. What kind of a fox just kills one chicken? I scanned the dark, snow-covered fields till I was satisfied there was no one out there. Then I lay down again. Waiting for Clem to come home was getting old; I was fit to be tied, having to sit tight until he showed up, and the whole thing was making me nervous and jumpy. My imagination was starting to get out of hand.

At table that morning we heard footsteps in the snow. Maggie was just setting a platter of flapjacks in front of me when a shadow darkened the kitchen window and a face peeked inside.

I fairly flew from my chair, thinking that surely this time Clem had returned. I whirled around, looking for Maggie's gun.

Eliza screamed and threw herself under the table. "Maggie! It was a bear stole the chicken!" she shrieked.

Maggie laughed, running right over to open the door. A huge black bear stomped in. Right away I saw Henry's hunting shirt beneath the bear's head, and Susannah standing right behind him, but Eliza's eyes were covered with her hands and she still crouched beneath the table, bawling something fierce.

"Pa, just look what you did!" Maggie scolded him, pointing to Eliza. Henry pulled back the bear's head, a pained look on his face. He slipped out of that bearskin as fast as he could, then crouched on all fours, peering under the table.

"Aw, come on now, 'Liza. Don't be afraid of my old bear coat!" he said, taking hold of the hide and spreading it out fur side down on the floor. "Looky here, child!"

Eliza peeked between her fingers at the old man as he drew a finger from the bear's nose along what would have been the belly all the way down to its tail.

"This here's where I cut him open. Then I split the skin on the inside of his hind legs and stripped it off his body." Henry stuck an arm into one of the front legs and wiggled his fingers out the other end. "The tricky part was not to split the front legs so they could be my sleeves! When I'd skinned those legs, I turned the hide and pulled it over them and the head. Took me the better part of a day!"

He ran his hand along the inside of the hide. I knelt down beside it and felt it too, then burrowed my fingers into the thick black fur on the head.

"I sprinkled salt on the inside and let my cow and my dogs lick it out," he continued. "When all that bear grease was licked clean out, I had me a winter coat with a hood. This old critter's kept me warm now almost forty years!"

Eliza laughed a little, looking foolish. "Where'd his claws go?" she asked.

"Ate 'em! Ain't nothin' tastes better than a bear's claw roasted in the embers of a dyin' fire. Wouldn't that be a Christmas treat!" Henry slapped his knee. "Course, there ain't been a bear around here since before Maggie was born."

I stroked that old bearskin from head to tail, wishing I could have known the wild young Missouri Henry had known. I thought how I'd rather fight off bears than my own neighbors and townsfolk.

For Christmas Susannah'd woven us each a wool coverlet, colored blue-purple with dye she'd made from blackberries. She slipped a necklace of hard corn kernels around Jimmy's neck. "To help him cut teeth," she explained.

The night before, Maggie'd hung up one of each of our socks, and slipped a few pieces of candy inside that she must've bought in Linneus when we weren't looking. Sometime between last night and breakfast, she'd put up an extra stocking too, a long one that hung empty.

Our Christmas supper sizzled and boiled, steaming all the windows and filling the house with a satisfying smell. Susannah'd just called us to table when there came a knock at the door. My heart jumped up into my throat, but I sat still. Maggie wiped a hole in the steam of the front window with a corner of her apron, peeking out before she opened it.

"It's Joel!" she cried, flinging open the door and throwing her arms around a brown-bearded man with spectacles perched on the end of his nose. He lifted Maggie off the ground, hugging her tight, then thumped across the room in snowy boots to kiss Susannah and shake hands with Henry.

Susannah grabbed a fistful of his whiskers and gently shook his head. "Son, it's powerful good to see yer face again!"

"Well now, Ma, how could I forget you and Pa on Christmas day? Or my baby sister? Peeling off his hat and coat, he handed them to Maggie. Then he noticed Eliza and me. "You takin' in boarders, Maggie?"

Before Maggie could answer, Susannah whisked the pipe from her mouth. "Refugees! Rebels chased 'em off their land down south of here."

Joel shook our hands, then flopped into the rocker. "Maggie always was a charitable soul. I'm proud to meet you both." Pulling off his spectacles, he began rubbing them dry with a handkerchief. "Well, I won't stay long; Ellen's waiting at home. We'll be eating our Christmas ham with her folks today. But there's a piece of news I mean to share with you all."

"Then out with it, boy." Henry drew up a stool across from his son and straddled it.

Joel Wilkinson cleared his throat. "Sheriff over in Linneus stepped down two weeks ago. Personal reasons, they say. Well, I been asked by the town council to take his place."

"Well, bless the Almighty, son!" Susannah drew herself up proud. "Ye'll be a fine sheriff, I dare say."

Joel slipped his spectacles back over his ears. He shook his head. "Ma, it's a job I don't want, particularly. Trying to keep the peace between folk bent on blastin' each other to kingdom come! Making sure the Vigilance Committee don't get out of hand! Shoot, before the war it might have been an easy job, but not now. Only the good Lord knows why they chose me."

"Ye've seen the wanted poster, son?" asked Henry.

"Pa!" Maggie snapped.

"Well, he's goin' to be sheriff, ain't he?"

"Yes, Pa, I know all about it," said Joel.

"Well, now ye're sheriff ye can hunt Clem down and bring him in. Ye can make him pay for what he done to yer little sister."

Joel stroked his beard and nodded thoughtfully. "He's wronged Maggie, that's sure, Pa. Runnin' off the way he done, bringin' shame on her and little Jimmy. Why, I was fit to chase him down and turn him in to the Yankees myself when I heard about all his doin's."

"Well, son," Henry said, nodding in a satisfied way, "I'll be proud to help ye when the time comes to take care of Clem."

Joel shook his head. "No, Pa. I ain't goin' to do it."

"What do ye mean ye ain't?" Henry's jaw nearly dropped into his lap.

"I mean Missouri's lost a heap too much blood already and someone's got to stop up the wound. Now I'm sheriff I reckon I can start. Could be that others hereabouts will follow me in it, least I hope they will."

Henry jumped to his feet, towering over his seated son. "It ain't a sheriff's job to stand in the way of justice!"

Maggie handed her brother a mug of cider, shaking so hard the drink sloshed out onto the floor. "Enough, Pa!"

Red in the face and curling his fingers into fists, Henry looked like any pa who was angry enough to snap off a hickory branch and peel it into a good sharp switch. "Lookit ye just sittin' there, Joel, saying ye'll let the likes of Clem go free! What kind of coward are ye to shirk your duty to the Union...and to Missouri?"

Joel raised himself up and stood eye to eye with his pa. His voice was steady. "My duty to Missouri, as I see it, is to stop the bloodlettin'."

"Then they oughtta make me sheriff! I'd bring that snivelin' oath-breaker in; I'd do my duty just as sure as ye won't!"

"Hush up, old man!" ordered Susannah. "No matter what ye or I think of Clem, he's Margaret's husband. Think on her!"

The old warrior clapped his mouth shut. He looked from Joel to Maggie to Susannah. Then, turning helplessly toward the fire, he sent an angry mouthful of spit sizzling into the flames. He sank down on the stool with his chin in both hands. "Our supper's gettin' cold," he grumbled.

Joel drained his cider mug dry. He set it down and crossed the room slowly to where his hat and coat hung. "I'll take my leave then, Pa."

Henry sat still, his eyes fixed on the fire. Joel leaned over and gave his ma a kiss, then took Maggie's hand in his. "He's a stubborn old cuss, but don't fret too much on his account," Joel said, loud enough for Henry to hear. "It's my guess he'll see things my way sooner or later."

Maggie hugged her brother good-bye, glaring at her pa over Joel's shoulder. Without another word she stomped off to the kitchen, not coming out again till supper was ready.

Pressing my forehead against the cold windowpane, I watched Joel ride up the snowy drive. I shook my head. It was a sad day when a Missouri sheriff wouldn't seek justice for a criminal. "Oh God," I prayed in a whisper, "let me get at that bushwhacker before he does." I let the curtain fall into place and walked over to where Henry sat on the hearth. Leaning over beside him, I spit into the flames just like he'd done. He and I were of the same mind.

We feasted on pork roast, potatoes, turnips, and corn, then had dried apple pie, molasses cake, and cider as we sat around the fire. The cider bit my tongue and tickled my throat, warming my gut as it went down. It recalled to my mind our Christmases at home and the sight of my pa bent over his cider press. The sweetest apple cider in Missouri ran trickling out of Pa's press. I could almost feel it now, cool and sticky on my fingers as I lapped it up and licked them clean. Pa always laughed, "Save some for your sisters, Jacob!"

Would Pa have cider to drink this Christmas? Even as I hoped so, my chest felt heavy and my heart wallowed deep down inside me. I closed my eyes. I could see Pa's upturned rocker glowing coal red in the ash heap that had been our home. Are you alive, Pa? And Ma, Sarah, Jerusha? Jerusha, so tiny I could barely remember her face. Lord, let them be alive somewhere!

When dinner was done, Henry sat on the hearth stool and fiddled, every now and then reaching down to swipe up some hickory sap oozing out of the burning log and lick it off his finger.

"Give me some, Henry!" sang out Eliza, bringing a spoon. "I want some hickory goody too!" He scraped her off a bite and blew on it till it hardened on the spoon like candy. Sitting on Henry's knee, Eliza sucked it slowly, contented, with her eyes half closed the way Susannah sucked her pipe.

Susannah rocked with Jimmy on her lap, holding up his tiny hands and chawing off the tips of his fingernails between her teeth. "If ye cut a child's nails with scissors he'll grow up to be a thief!" she declared. I peeked over at Maggie knitting in the stuffed chair. She rolled her eyes and I looked down quick to hide my smile.

Henry put his fiddle to his chin, closed his eyes, and sang,

> Cold on his cradle the dewdrops are shinin',
> Low lies his head with the beasts of the stall.
> Angels adore him in slumber reclinin',
> Maker, and monarch and savior of all.

Brightest and best of the sons of the mornin',
Dawn on our darkness and lend us thine aid,
Star of the East, the horizon adornin',
Guide where our infant redeemer is laid.

With a knife Maggie'd loaned me, I finished up the little hickory bowl I'd been whittling of an evening. I stole upstairs and wrapped it in a page from an old *Linneus Bulletin,* hiding it under my bed. Suddenly what I'd just done seemed foolish. "You ought to take that out and just give it to Maggie," I told myself. But I couldn't do it. I'd given to my own ma everything I'd whittled before. To give it to Maggie just didn't seem right.

When I'd crept back downstairs and sat down to crack nuts on the hearth rug, Henry nudged me with his foot. "Yer stocking's hangin' a heap lower than the others, boy. I guess there's somethin' inside." I jumped up and ran to it, reaching my fingers way down until I felt something cold and hard. "Careful of the edges!" he warned.

Out came a tomahawk forged of iron, with steel edges. I ran my fingers slowly along the smooth side of the blade.

"That war hatchet once belonged to a Sauk Indian," Henry told me. "He most likely traded for it with settlers, for it's made by a white man."

The notion that it had been in the hands of an Indian made my chest swell up and my heart beat wild. "And it's mine?"

"Yes, boy, take it. I found it amongst some of my old things. An old man like me don't need more than one tommyhawk anyway." He patted the one that always hung from his belt.

I felt like Sauk blood rushed through me then, and for the first time since being bushwhacked, all that I'd buried inside me came bursting out. I ran to the front door and out into the yard that was all lit up by a thick fall of snow. "Yi yi yi yi yi!" I screamed, sounding as much like an Indian as I could, for I'd never seen or heard one. I sent that tomahawk spinning through the air until it landed with a thud in the side of an elm tree. The family gathered on the porch as I leaped to pry it loose. They watched me run circles in the snow, whirling and swinging that war hatchet above my head and screeching like a warrior. Old Henry laughed out loud and slapped his knee. Susannah smiled down at me, puffing on her pipe, the baby in her arms. Maggie stood with her hands on her hips, shaking her head, and behind her Eliza peered out at me from the front window's steamy glass.

"You'll be as wild as my brothers, Jacob!" Maggie scolded, but I could tell she wasn't mad.

As I made my way up the stairs at bedtime, I looked down to see Maggie take down the long, empty sock she'd hung up the night before. With her head hanging, she curled it up slowly, and I knew then she'd hung it for Clem.

Lying in bed beneath our new wool coverlets, Eliza asked me if our folks were keeping warm, like she did almost every night. And like I did each time she asked, I said, yes, I thought they were.

"But Jacob, I still don't understand why they up and went to Iowa without us."

Breathing deep, I steadied myself by letting the air out slow. She'd asked the same question so many times since that night last October! Now my patience was running thin, like my hope, but I forced out the words again—words I was having a harder and harder time believing myself.

"Now, you know Pa had to run to save his neck," I repeated for the hundredth time. "Those bushwhackers would have killed

The family watched me run circles in the snow, whirling and swinging that war hatchet above my head and screeching like a warrior.

him for sure if he'd come back there again. He and Ma must have made their way north to Aunt Lucille's, thinkin' we'd follow. And we will, Eliza, once spring comes."

As always, those words calmed my sister and put her to sleep.

But I couldn't get those shivering, ragged refugees out of my mind, sleeping in worn-out army tents, and under wagon boxes. Were my folks somewhere in Missouri, living like them? Or were they even alive to feel cold and hunger?

I reached under my pillow to where I'd hid my tomahawk and fell asleep with one hand on the cool iron blade.

S now lay like a thin-worn quilt over the hills. It piled up
thick along the sides of the road. Long tufts of brown
prairie grass stuck out of it and lay flat in the wind.

Like all God's creatures, we turned our hands to surviving.
Alongside Henry and his hounds, I tramped my new boots all
over Locust Creek Country, hunting rabbit, squirrel, and deer.
The week after Christmas Henry brought down a nice doe with
his old flintlock, and that meat filled our bellies for a good
while after.

We ate corn until I wondered if I'd ever want to set my eyes
on another cob again. At breakfast Maggie boiled us up cornmeal mush and milk. At noontime we had cornbread alongside
our meat, and at suppertime parched corn. Sometimes she grit-
ted a dry ear of corn over the rough side of a piece of tin all
studded with nail holes. She'd boil the grits up into a thick paste
we'd pour molasses on or eat with butter and salt. On Sunday
evenings she'd fry up corn fritters in the spider pan; midweek
we'd eat a succotash with kernels of corn floating around
among the salt pork and beans.

"Be thankful for it, boy!" scolded Henry one evening when
I turned up my nose at the bowl of parched corn Maggie set
before me. "Mother corn kept me alive my first few winters here

in Missouri. The Indians worshipped her; they knew what she was worth!"

I spooned an extra thick layer of molasses on it and ate it up, feeling ashamed. But I could just about taste the squash and the green beans and the soft wheat bread my ma used to bake.

One day, when we were pretty well set for the winter and the weather had turned bitter, Maggie decided she might as well send Eliza and me to the schoolhouse down on the Linneus road. She herself had learned to read and write there, she told us.

"There's no sense in you and your sister growin' fat and lazy inside the house all day. Your ma would want you to keep up with your book learnin'," she said, and I had to admit Ma probably would. But when we'd trudged the half mile there one morning through the snow, all we found was an empty building with the door nailed shut. Henry told us later he'd heard the schoolteacher had gone and joined the Union army barely a week before.

Henry and Susannah spent a good many evenings at Maggie's fireside. Henry'd bring along a *Linneus Bulletin* and hand it to me or Maggie, asking us to read the war news on account of he couldn't read much more than the labels on the goods he sold in his store. That's how we learned that "Old Pap"—that is, Confederate General Price—and his men had fallen back to Springfield and set up winter quarters. Henry'd heard travelers say the Confederate hero's men pretty much did as they pleased, not paying heed to their superiors or even properly keeping watch against the enemy. Well, what could you expect from a pompous old general who spent all his time drinking whiskey, Henry said. The South could have him and Henry was glad they did.

I guess Susannah meant well, but she persecuted poor Eliza something awful on those winter evenings. And though I pitied my sister I couldn't help but think she deserved it. The old woman would carry a basket of wool up to the house, then expect Eliza to pick the burrs out of it along with her. Other nights Susannah'd hover over Eliza, making sure she learned the proper way to darn a sock or sew a seam. Eliza chafed and fussed, saying she'd been accustomed to doing her embroidery in the evenings, but Susannah threw her hands in the air and declared she didn't know what good fancy needlework would do her if Eliza couldn't even sew a pillowcase to lay her head on.

"What could have possessed yer ma all these years, to let you grow up ignorant of a woman's work?" fussed Susannah one February night as she lit the oil lamp for Eliza to sew by. Eliza scowled and set her hand to sewing, but with just about every stitch she heaved a big sigh and squirmed in her seat.

I lay by the fire trying to read the *Bulletin* out loud to Henry, but I could hardly stick my eyes to the print what with all the ruckus Susannah was making over Eliza's rushed and careless stitching. She'd snatch the cloth out of my sister's hand, scolding her and ripping out the thread. Then she'd say, "Look here!" and make her watch the proper way to do it. Along about the third time that happened, Eliza's fury came busting out for all to see.

"I ain't goin' to keep fussin' with this thing!" Eliza hollered, throwing the cloth, needle, and thread onto the woodpile and jumping up off her chair. Her thimble clattered to the floor and bounced into a dark corner. Calhoun bolted and chased the tiny thing like it was a rabbit.

"My ma never made me do it and you can't neither!" Eliza yelled.

Across the room, Maggie sprang to her feet. Grabbing up a kindling stick, she made straight for Eliza. When my sister saw what was coming, she screamed and tried to back her behind against the wall, but not quick enough. All at once Maggie got hold of Eliza's arm, wheeled her around, and smacked her good and hard on the backside. Then she threw down the stick and clasped hold of Eliza's shoulders, giving her a shake.

"Now listen here, child," she scolded. "I went soft and easy on you when you first came, 'cause you were sick. Now you're well. You ought to be pullin' your weight! It ain't my fault you know next to nothin' about keepin' house, but now you're under my roof and I aim to see you learn. And you'd best learn it all while you're young. A woman who can't keep house finds herself in a bad fix in this world, and I'll be hanged if I'm gonna let that happen to you!"

Eliza's cheeks glowed red as the fire. Rubbing her backside, she slowly turned and shuffled back to her chair, where Calhoun waited with the thimble he'd hunted down. He dropped it, all slobbered up, at her feet, then crouched, barely taking his muzzle off it, waiting for her to throw it again. I buried my face behind the newspaper, knowing I had to choke back my laughter. Eliza'd been humiliated enough already.

Late that night when I was near to falling asleep, Eliza sat up on the crackling husks and pulled her knees up to her chin. "I guess you're glad I got a lickin' tonight, ain't you, Jacob?" she whispered. "Well, I'm gonna tell you somethin'. I ain't mad at Maggie." She looked down at me, and I could see by the moonlight on her face that she expected me to say something.

"Ain't you?" was all I could think of.

"No," she said. "No, and here's why. I know I been lazy. And I think havin' Maggie's almost as good as havin' a ma.

Since I can't have my ma right now...I'm glad I have Maggie."
Having spoke her peace, she lay back down and went to sleep,
with me following right behind.

A sharp cackling awoke me in the dead of night.

"The chickens!" I blurted out, throwing off my covers and
running for the stairs. Maggie came down the steps right behind
me, but I'd grabbed up her gun from the mantel and was out the
kitchen door before she reached the bottom step. Standing in the
moonlit yard, I watched Calhoun's tail end bounding over the
snowy field toward the creek. Once again he hadn't barked,
hadn't warned us what was coming.

I started off toward the henhouse, but Maggie was right
behind me. She grabbed me by the nightshirt. "I'll check for
tracks, Jacob."

"Let me!" I cried.

"No! Now you go on inside and build up the fire. Ain't no
sense goin' back to bed now. It's almost chore time."

My eyes wandered over her shoulder to the henhouse and I
took a step in that direction. She crossed her arms and stood her
ground, blocking my way.

Slowly I turned and went inside. That crazy woman!

While she tended to the chickens, I went to the barn to feed
the livestock and get what little milk I could from the cow.
Leaning up close to her warm flank, I wondered how long the
snow would hold. Spring and good traveling weather couldn't
come soon enough for me. Whether or not my folks were alive,
I figured Iowa was where Eliza and I belonged. I began to count
the weeks until we could go there.

Crossing the yard with the bucket of milk, I glanced out
across the fields. A lone horseman sat still on a rise, a rifle bal-
anced across his lap. He turned his head slowly, scanning the

hills. I'd seen him before in the early mornings, though I hadn't known who he was until one cold clear dawn when the sun caught and flashed off his spectacles. It was Maggie's brother, Joel Wilkinson. I stood watching him as I breathed the stinging cold air into my nose. He seemed to be waiting for something, waiting silent and still like a hunter waits for a deer. Finally he turned his horse and disappeared into a draw.

When I'd finished my chores I hurried back to the chicken yard, but if any tracks had been left, they'd been so kicked around and filled in with blowing snow I couldn't read them. Only Calhoun's paw prints were clear as day, running off toward the woods.

After two days the dog still hadn't come back.

"I think Calhoun stole the chickens," I told Maggie as she washed up the dinner dishes.

She laughed. "Calhoun's no thief."

"Then where'd he go?"

She took awhile to answer. "Guess he chased that old fox. Maybe tangled with him."

"It wasn't no fox, Maggie!" I declared, exasperated. "Everyone knows a fox don't just take one hen and run off, leavin' the place all neat and tidy! And now we're down to five hens."

Maggie slammed a plate down so hard a piece chipped off. "Jacob, don't concern yourself with it! We'll get by. Calhoun's somewhere nearby. I can feel it. Please don't worry."

When after two more days Calhoun still hadn't come home, I decided to hunt for him. I pulled my tomahawk out from under my pillow and stuck it in my belt, setting off across the fields toward Locust Creek. When I reached the edge of the creek woods I cupped my hands around my mouth.

"Calhoun!" I called. A bobwhite flapped up out of the brush, but no dog came running. As my eyes followed the line of naked oaks, birches, and hickories snaking their way north along the edge of the Locust, I thought how I'd follow them up to Iowa one day, just as soon as spring came.

I moved into the woods and called for Calhoun again. This time I got an answer. I knew it was Calhoun, though it was just one quick bark coming from down ahead in the ravine. Thinking he might be lying hurt, I quickened my steps, cracking twigs and dead leaves beneath the snow as I went.

I stopped clean when I caught the smell of smoke. I looked around me at the bare trees, confused, for I hadn't seen any sign of a fire when I'd crossed the field. Then again, smoke rising up from the creek bottom would hang low in the trees on a still day like this, hiding itself against the ash-gray clouds. Curling my fingers around the handle of my war hatchet, I half slid downhill toward the creek bottom.

Then I saw the fire. It burned low in a ditch, and rocks were piled around it. I stiffened up and drew in a sharp breath. Beside the fire stood a tall, ragged man with a rifle aimed right at me. Calhoun was at his side. Through the gun sights the man gazed good and long at me and my little old tomahawk, then lowered the rifle slowly and propped it against a fallen log. He stooped to pick up something—a cottontail rabbit, all limp and bloodied. I figured he must have dropped it when he'd gone for his gun.

"You skeered me!" he drawled, pulling a shiny, two-edged knife from his belt. Squatting by the fire, he set to skinning his kill, while Calhoun bounded straight for me, jumping up and licking my hand. I stroked his neck, never taking my eyes off the stranger.

The man glanced up at me as he worked. "You can come closer. I ain't gonna hurt you."

Afraid to go nearer, but knowing I'd look a fool if I turned and ran, I inched my way toward the fire. A hickory stump barely two yards from it made a good stopping place; I sat down, circling both arms around Calhoun. He pushed his nose into my neck and whimpered.

The stranger skinned the rabbit with his long, curved blade, and I could see it was a bowie knife with a polished horn handle. He cut the skin from the flesh in short, jerking movements, his eyes darting here and there. His body tensed up at every little rustling sound coming out of the woods. Only after turning his head in a long, slow circle would he hunch down again over his kill.

His hat was all ragged around the edges and looked like a crow's nest turned upside down. Beneath it his hair hung long and straight, matted with dirt and grease. He had a wild look about him, like he'd been living in fields and woods so long he'd become a part of them. His wrists hung out of coat sleeves that were shrunken and wrinkled like they'd been soaked and dried in the sun too many times. Most of all, he looked tired. His dark eyes were rimmed underneath with black circles, and I thought I saw the hand that held the knife tremble.

Steam rose from the rabbit's hot blood as he cut it open and hacked the shiny pink flesh into chunks. He speared one on a stick, looking up at me.

"Come here, boy," he said, offering me a piece of meat. The blood dripped through his dirty fingers, splattering the snow beneath. I held back a minute. Then I reached out and took the meat. The corner of his mouth twitched up in a little smile beneath his overgrown mustache.

"Come here, boy," he said, offering me a piece of meat.

I speared my meat on a stick of my own and began to roast it. The outside turned black before the inside cooked all the way, but the hungry man yanked his off the stick and tore his teeth into it, hardly caring that the juice ran down his arms and into his coat sleeves. When Calhoun whined and lay his muzzle on the stranger's knee, the man hacked off a chunk of raw rabbit flesh and fed it to him.

As I ate, my eyes wandered around the makeshift camp. On a nearby rock lay a cloth haversack and a bedroll with dead leaves and twigs stuck to it. Chicken feathers—red-brown like Maggie's hens—lay scattered on the snow. Stretched between two stick poles and tied on with prairie grass, a rabbit skin dried near the fire, a light breeze ruffling its clean-scrubbed fur.

When the rabbit's carcass had been stripped bare, the stranger tossed it into the creek. Now that his belly was full he seemed to relax, strolling down to the water's edge to wash his hands and his knife. After scraping the fat off and scrubbing the bloody rabbit's skin, he returned to the fire, untying the dried skin from the poles and replacing it with the wet one. Then he rolled up the dry skin and tossed it on top of his haversack. Sitting down on a log across the fire pit from me, he held his hands out to dry and stared at me through the flames.

"She takin' good care of you?" he asked.

His question gave me a start, but I took care not to show it. "Yes sir, she is."

"She's a good woman. The girl's yer sister?"

"Yes sir."

He nodded. Just then some jays flapped up out of the grass at the top of the bank. The man jerked up his head, reaching for his gun, his eyes sweeping across the skeleton trees on the rim of the bank. Nothing moved. Only a woodpecker's hammering echoed through the trees. Satisfied that all was still, he stood up and reached for the rabbit skin sitting atop his haversack. He rolled it up, then stroked it once, gently.

"Give this to Margaret," he said, tossing it to me. "I reckon she can sew herself a pair of gloves."

Just as I caught it, a horse's whinny came from the top of the bank, followed by the sound of a rifle being cocked. The stranger wheeled around and stepped toward his gun, but stopped when he saw Joel Wilkinson's rifle trained on him. He raised his hands high and sank to his knees in the snow.

Stranger in the House

The sheriff swung a leg slowly over his saddle and dropped to the ground, still holding his aim. He let out a long, low whistle. "Don't you look a sight, Clement Canaday!"

The bedraggled bushwhacker blinked hard and stared up at Joel a second or two, like he couldn't quite get his wits together. He drew the back of his hand across his dirty face and sniffed. "I reckon I do."

Joel moved down the snowy bank with slow, careful steps till he wasn't but five yards or so from his prisoner. He smiled. "Been awhile, ain't it, Clem?"

The outlaw nodded.

"The folks in Linneus gone and made me sheriff."

Clem raised his eyebrows. "That a fact?"

Calhoun broke away from me then and ran to his master. He snarled, baring teeth at the sheriff. Taking a step in Joel's direction, then turning back to circle Clem, he came around again to face the captor. But even he seemed to understand that a man with a firearm has the upper hand. Whining helplessly, he licked Clem's upraised palm.

Joel lowered his rifle, keeping its muzzle trained on Clem. "Fetch me his gun, Jacob."

Like coming out of a long sleep, I looked from Joel to Clem, then back to Joel again. I let the rabbit skin slip out of my fingers and watched it fall onto the snow. What in damnation had I been doing, sitting sharing meat with a bushwhacker? Hadn't I known it was Clem all along, starting the minute I saw Calhoun all friendly with him? I jumped up off my hickory stump and went for his rifle. When I grabbed it I could feel Clem's eyes on me and my legs went weak, nearly making me lose my balance in the snow. Then the idea struck me to snatch up Clem's haversack. As soon as I felt its weight I knew I'd done right. At the bottom of the sack lay a Navy pistol, along with a whole mess of pistol caps and paper cartridges.

"He's got a bowie knife under his coat," I whispered, handing the haversack to Joel.

"That true, Clem?" he asked. "You got a bowie knife too? Throw it here."

The outlaw obeyed, tossing the knife at my feet, where it sank deep in the snow. I snatched it up quick and dropped it in the sack. A rush of excitement swelled inside me. Of course Joel didn't mean what he said at Maggie's on Christmas day! He meant to take Clem in and see him hang, just like a sheriff ought to.

"Had a feelin' you'd come crawlin' back home again when the winter got hard," said Joel. "Huntin' been scarce?"

Clem lifted sad, empty eyes. He nodded.

"I got one question for you," Joel continued, moving a step closer. "Would you be wantin' to go home for good now, Clem? To farm your land again, and live with your wife and boy?"

Clem opened his mouth to speak, but his lips trembled so hard the words wouldn't come. A sudden wind whistled up the creek bed, blowing his hair across his eyes. "I would surely love to see Margaret again," he mumbled.

"But will you stay, Clem?" Joel persisted.

"You sound like a preacher at a weddin'." Clem smirked.

"I said do you aim to stay on your farm!" Joel's voice shot out, echoing through the woods and scaring the woodpecker into silence.

The Rebel wiped the smirk off his face quick enough. "I reckon so, Joel," he answered. "If she'll have me."

"All right, then, listen up good." Joel dropped down on one knee till he was eye to eye with Clem. He lay his rifle across his knee, keeping his finger on the trigger. "Now, you had no right to burn Asa Wheeler's house down, but that's none of the Yankees' business. I'm sheriff here, and I'll see to it you make amends."

"I ain't—" interrupted Clem, but Joel kept right on talking.

"And I don't know why you took a notion to turn Rebel, but nothin' you did was worth hangin' you for, in my opinion. The provost marshal's a friend of mine. I've been tellin' him I thought you'd come home one of these days, and that I was sure you'd make no more trouble for the Federals if you were given half a chance to settle down. It just so happens he owes me a favor, and he's takin' my word on you, Clem. If you'll come in and take the oath again he'll give you your chance."

Clem shut his eyes, the muscles in his face pulling tight. He looked to be in pain just from listening to Joel's words.

"He's got business down in Laclede today," Joel said. "Now, nobody's gonna recognize you down there, what with your hair grown all long like that. You let me haul you down there to take the oath again, and you'll be a free man. Can't promise how safe you'll be. But you'll be free. I got a feeling if you lie low on your own farm awhile, the whole ugly mess will just blow over."

Clem shook his head violently. He locked his hands together above his head and pressed his hat down flat. He stared down at his knees a long time, wrestling with himself so hard I could almost feel it from where I stood.

"It's the only way, Clem!" Joel insisted. "Take the oath again...for Maggie's sake."

"I'd be a liar, twice over," protested the outlaw.

"No, no, Clem," persuaded the sheriff, more kindly now. "You aim to lay down arms, don't you? To make no more trouble for the Union?"

"I ain't gonna swear loyalty to the Yankee nation!"

Joel sighed like he'd run out of patience. He got to his feet. "You run off and left your wife and baby! You burnt down Asa Wheeler's house and stole his horse! Made Maggie ashamed to show her face in town, after what you done. Then you ran wild with Rebel ruffians, makin' yourself a stench to the Union army in these parts! If you run off again, Clem, you'll get no chance to go back. The Federals hang oath-breakers! Will you leave your wife and son to bear the shame of it?"

The bushwhacker folded his head down beneath his locked hands and bent low until his filthy hair dragged in the snow. He rocked miserably from side to side, mumbling to himself. For the first time I noticed his boots were too small. He'd cut slits for his toes to stick out, and his wool stockings were sopping wet from soaking up snow. I looked down at my own new boots, then away. He wasn't getting near what he deserved, I reminded myself. He's just like the thieving scoundrels who burned down our house. "Lord, don't let Clem say yes," I pleaded. "Don't let him go free!"

The crunch of Joel's boots in the snow brought my head around again. The sheriff set the toe of his boot under Clem's chin and lifted his head. "Your little boy's a handsome fellow, Clem. Don't you want to see him grow up? If you don't take that oath, I can't help you. You understand?"

Clem stared past Joel into the silent sky. The woodpecker started in tapping again, filling the empty silence of the woods. I waited for the outlaw's reply. Finally he nodded his head.

Joel re-aimed his gun. "All right then. Stand up." Hands still on his hat, Clem struggled to his feet. "There's a rope in my saddlebag, Jacob." Joel nodded toward his horse. "You bring it on down."

I hesitated. What was Joel doing? A sheriff ought to haul an outlaw in to jail, not take pains to get him pardoned.

"Go on, boy, do as I say," said Joel.

Numbly I did what I was told. Clem offered his hands to be tied up with one end of the rope, then let Joel lead him up the bank and loop the other end around his saddle horn.

Joel smiled. "I'd offer you a ride, Clem, but I don't exactly trust you. Yet." He mounted his horse and led his prisoner away through the snowy woods. With my arms full of Clem's weapons, I climbed the bank and watched him stumble along at the rope's end, across his own snowy fields toward the road to Laclede. Watching him go, an angry fire kindled up inside me and burst into flame. I stood there, my hands tight around Clem's rifle, my teeth grinding together so hard my jaw hurt. How could I just stand there and let him get away? Yet when I tried to lift my legs they felt heavier than blacksmith's anvils.

Calhoun trotted alongside his master as far as the road, but there Clem twisted himself around. "Git on home!" he snapped. The dog stopped at the road's edge, whimpering. By the time I reached Calhoun, Clem wasn't much more than a small speck where the sky met the earth. Calhoun began to whine.

"Hush up!" I screamed. He yapped and jumped up on me, trying to lick my face. "Get off." I shoved him away with the butt of Clem's rifle. "You fool dog! Don't you know what he is?"

Flinging Clem's haversack to the ground, I raised the gun to my shoulder. Through the gunsights, Clem was no more than the size of a pea rolling down the road, but I drew a bead on him just the same. I fired. The shot echoed across the empty hills and threw me backward into the snow. Between my own trembling and Calhoun's jumping at me I knew I'd shot thin air.

"No!" I crawled toward the haversack and thrust my hand inside, fumbling for a cartridge. But by the time I shoved it into the gun barrel with the ramrod, Clem was gone. I hurled both rifle and ramrod across the road and into the banked-up snow on its other side. Sinking to my knees, I hunched forward, punching the frozen earth with both fists and howling like a trap-caught wolf. Calhoun stuck his wet nose in my ear and licked my face, trying to comfort me.

The whole time I'd been in his camp, the bushwhacker had never been more than a stone's throw away from me. Yet I'd let him walk away. Sure, his hands were tied up. But he was tied to a sheriff bent on turning him loose.

"I ought to have scalped him while I had the chance, Calhoun!" I raged. The fool dog cocked his head and looked sorry for me. I shook my head and cursed myself. Why hadn't I tricked Clem? Why didn't I steal his gun when he wasn't looking? If only Joel hadn't turned up when he did! Curse that fool sheriff with all his talk about binding up Missouri's bleeding wounds!

Clutching fistfuls of hair on either side of my head, I flopped face down in the snow. So Joel was going to get Clem pardoned. Then what? Then Clem'd come home. Come home to his wife and baby to pick up his plow, just like Henry'd said. But he'd be coming home to someone else, too. Jacob Knight. Yes, I'd be there, biding my time, and when my chance came, I'd take it. Hadn't I made a deal with Johann Metzger and Asa Wheeler?

I hauled myself up and tramped across the road to collect Clem's rifle. "Come on, Calhoun!" I called, wiping my face on my coat sleeve. Then I made my way up to the house to tell Maggie what I'd seen.

~

Clem was back home again by the next afternoon. Eliza, sitting at the quilting frame by the front window, saw him first and came bursting out the back door to the woodpile where I was busy chopping.

"He's comin', Jacob!" she panted, her freckled face all tight with fear. I grabbed hold of her arm and squeezed as tight as I dared.

"Now hush!" I told her. "Clem ain't gonna hurt you, 'cause I won't let him. He ain't gonna hurt anyone."

"How do you know that?" she asked, trying to yank her arm free.

"Because I've got a plan and I've worked it all out, and you got to trust your big brother. Now just stay quiet and don't let him know you're afraid!" I let go of her arm and went inside to call upstairs to Maggie.

She came running down with Jimmy on her hip, her face white as the snowy fields. When she threw open the front door, Calhoun burst out and raced down the drive, his tail almost fit to fly off of him, he was wagging it so hard. When Maggie saw her brother and husband riding up to the house on Joel's horse, she covered her mouth with her hand and sank against the door frame. Both men dismounted a good ten yards off from the porch. With Jimmy straddling her hip and pulling on her hair,

Maggie straightened herself up and stepped outside to meet her husband. Eliza and I pulled back inside the doorway to watch.

Tired-looking and dirty, Clem strolled to the bottom of the steps. He passed a rough, bony hand over his face as if to wipe away his shame, then let it dangle, useless, at his side. He just stood there, smelling like horse manure, gazing up at his wife and son, until Joel came up behind him and clapped a hand on his shoulder. Clem took a deep breath and let it out slow. He pressed his lips together and opened his eyes wide, the way folk do when they're trying hard to stop tears from coming.

"It's me been stealin' yer chickens, Margaret."

Maggie swayed from side to side, rocking her baby. "I figured as much, Clem. It don't matter. They're your chickens, well as mine."

"I couldn't come up to the house," he went on. "I didn't want to make no trouble for you."

She looked down at her skirt. With trembling fingers, she smoothed down some hairs that Jimmy'd pulled loose from the knot at the back of her head.

"I know I ain't presentable," continued Clem. "I been in jail down in Laclede this night, and couldn't clean myself up. But will you have a weary traveler to supper?"

"That depends," Maggie answered, swinging Jimmy over to her other hip.

"What on?"

"On if your bushwhackin' days are over. 'Cause if they ain't you can just turn around and go back to the Laclede jail."

Clem scratched his head, looking past Maggie up to the porch roof. He wiggled his stuck-out toes and scraped one boot heel across the bottom step a few times. "Yeah. Yeah, Margaret. They're over."

"There's one more thing," she added. "I've taken in children. Jacob and Eliza are winterin' here. You got to accept it."

"I know. And I do."

"Well then." Maggie blushed a little and looked at her feet. "I guess our business is settled." She gave Clem a nod, and he walked up the steps and into the house. At sight of him disappearing into that doorway, Eliza took a stranglehold on my arm and buried her face in my shirtsleeve. I made myself stand tall and straight as I could, keeping my chin stiff.

"I'm grateful, Joel," said Maggie.

The sheriff waved away his sister's thanks. "I did what I saw fit to do, kin or no kin."

Maggie nodded. She turned and followed her husband inside. I looked long and hard at Joel Wilkinson. "You want Clem's weapons?" I tried to make my voice come out calm and civil.

"Naw, Jacob. I guess he'll need 'em."

"Yes sir," I whispered. The sheriff mounted his horse then and rode off, looking to me like he didn't care one bit that he'd left me and my sister to live with a thieving Rebel bushwhacker. I watched him go, wondering what kind of man he was to turn loose a barn-burning scoundrel like Clem. What sorry lot had made him sheriff, anyway? Good men must be as scarce as good horses in Missouri these days, I told myself.

"Yes, that's it," I said to no one in particular, though Eliza hung on to me, sobbing into my shirtsleeve. "The good horses and the good men are all used up, and there ain't nothin' but nags and fool cowards left."

~

Clem was a quiet man. That first day home, he sat meekly while Maggie cut off his hair and scrubbed his head with cider vinegar and egg yellows to kill the vermin. Dressed in a clean homespun shirt and pants and wearing his worn-heeled work boots again, he looked like any farmer in those parts. But Maggie's soft soap couldn't wash away the dark circles below his eyes, nor the lonely, hunted look in them.

Sleep came hard for me those first few days after Clem showed up. That first night, he and Maggie sat up till nigh midnight. I could hear her scolding and crying something awful, and in between Clem mumbled a word here and there, apologizing, I'd guess. The following nights, Clem sat up alone, watching the fire die down before he made his way up to bed. I lay open-eyed long after crawling under my quilt, aching something awful for my lost family, knowing the bushwhacker was awake downstairs. On those nights I pulled my tomahawk close, curling and uncurling my fingers around its smooth-carved handle.

On the fourth night I lay still, listening to Maggie climb the stairs with Jimmy. She sang him to sleep behind the closed door of her room. When she didn't go back down I knew she'd lain down to rest alongside her baby. I lifted my head and turned toward Eliza. The dark outline of her body rose up and sank down slowly with her quiet breath. Somewhere outside an owl hooted. I slid my hand under my pillow. When my fingers found the tomahawk, my heart nearly rushed out of my mouth and I had to gulp and gasp to keep it back down.

Slowly I folded back my cover and swung my legs to the floor. The cold night air hit me with a shudder. Moving toward the door my legs felt slow and heavy, like they were dragging through a dead hawthorn thicket. Nice and easy, I pulled the door open and slipped my head and shoulder through.

There he was, sitting in the stuffed chair with his back toward me, his long legs stretched out toward the dying fire. An oil lamp flickering on the mantel sent the shadow of his head rushing to meet me halfway up the stairs. Sliding the war hatchet between the folds of my nightshirt, I moved silently down the steps, shaking so hard my teeth rattled. Through the pounding of blood in my head, I heard the mantel clock tick louder as I drew closer to it.

A sudden snore from Clem jerked me backward in surprise. I stood still to catch my breath, relieved to know he slept. My hand gripped my weapon tighter. Closing my eyes, I made the journey one more time—the one I'd made a thousand times since the night we were bushwhacked. There it was, the way I liked to see it: our farm back in Howard County. Its summer wheat swayed back and forth beneath a cloudless sky, and I could hear Ma whistling as she hung the wash. Pa was brushing down a horse in the barn, while Eliza and Sarah climbed across the hay bales, chattering and picking straw out of their braids.

I shivered. Gunfire exploded in my head. Ma screamed. Fire, hungry and red, rushed through it all, eating up my home and family, eating up my heart and soul. Clem's head was so close now I could see the little hairs Maggie'd just trimmed on the back of his neck. His shoulders rose and fell with each breath he took.

I raised the tomahawk. Higher I brought it, and still higher, to give me a stronger blow. Trembling, I took my aim, but a squeak on the stairs behind me made me loosen my grip.

"Jacob!" hissed Eliza. "No!"

I jerked my head toward her, nearly dropping the tomahawk. Quickly I glanced back at Clem. He snorted, stirred, then slumped down again, his chin on his chest. I raised my weapon a second time, but Eliza was on me like a sharp-clawed hawk on a rabbit. Grabbing my raised arm with both her hands, she jerked me back with all her might, bringing me down on top of her.

I raised my weapon a second time, but Eliza was on me
like a sharp-clawed hawk on a rabbit.

Clem coughed. I held Eliza down, hardly daring to draw breath till I saw his head drop down again. "Let me be!" I whispered, struggling to my feet. I jerked my arm away from her but she found it again and sunk her fingernails into my flesh.

"No, Jacob! Maggie's upstairs. You can't."

"I can! She don't need him!"

"We need Maggie, Jacob. What'll happen to us if you kill her husband? She's like…she's like a ma to us now."

"I don't care." I shoved her aside so hard she lost her balance and fell thumping on the floor.

Another cough made me hush. Clem's head was up now. He slid forward on the seat and stretched slowly up to his full height. Eliza jumped to her feet and stepped in front of me. I buried the tomahawk in the folds of my nightshirt just before he turned and saw us.

Clem drew his thumb and fingers together over his tired eyes. "It's late. Fire's about dead," he yawned.

"Yes sir," I replied.

"You all ought to be in bed."

"Yes sir," said Eliza. "We wanted…water."

Clem crossed to the mantel and put out the lamp. "Well, you kids get upstairs. Go on."

I cursed under my breath as I mounted the stairs behind Eliza. But as I slid the tomahawk back beneath my pillow, I knew that she was right. Maggie had been good to me. There was no doubt in my mind she'd be better off without an outlaw like Clem for a husband, but it wouldn't do for me to be the one to lay a hand on him. There were others, eager as I was, to see him brought down. I'd let them do the job.

～

Before long the weather warmed up considerable, bringing on an early thaw. Maggie informed Eliza that it was spring housecleaning time for the womenfolk. My eyes nearly popped out of my head when I saw Eliza emptying out the cupboards and scrubbing them inside, then scrubbing the floors from corner to corner. She didn't sing or smile while she was doing it, but she didn't whine either. She only scowled at me a time or two as I passed by.

Clem took his time getting back to his chores. The first week he was home he wandered out on the front porch now and then, leaning over the railing and closing his eyes, like he just wanted to smell the slow-thawing fields. Then he'd go back inside and sit by the fire, whittling a little oak horse for Jimmy. Me, I sweat beneath my coat as I ran to and fro between the dripping eaves of the house and barn. I tarred cracks in the barn walls and patched holes in its roof before another snow came, as I knew one surely would. February always brought a few deceitful days with it, making folk think spring had come when it really hadn't. Even the coons were fooled; they woke up from their winter's sleep and began hunting up food. Calhoun caught one sneaking around the henhouse one night and raised such a yelping fuss that Clem jumped out of bed, grabbed his rifle, and threw open his bedroom window.

"Get off my land, you thievin' Yankees!" he screamed. I bolted upright in bed, my heart pounding. Soon all fell quiet. Next morning, we found the dead coon in the yard, and Calhoun had plenty of scratches to show for the fight he'd won. Clem didn't say a word, just skinned his dog's kill and nailed the hide up on the barn wall to dry.

Our lives went on mostly the same as before, only Henry and Susannah left off coming up to Maggie's house of an evening. After bringing Clem home to Maggie, Henry said Joel had ridden straight to his folks' cabin. He'd warned his pa not to make trouble, so the old man stayed put. I missed the old fiddling, storytelling warrior, and whenever I got the chance I'd steal on up the road to see him.

"Didn't I warn ye?" Henry railed the first time I went. "Didn't I say that Rebel fool son-in-law of mine would come back here?" He squatted near his hearth, rubbing cooled ashes on his boots to blacken them. "Well, I want no part of him. Joel wasted his breath warnin' me to stay away, 'cause I'd just as soon curse myself as shake his hand!"

Susannah stirred a boiling pot of onion skins hanging over the fire. Her mouth turned down at the corners and her eyes had lost their shine. "I'd be proud to shake Clem's hand if only I could see my Margaret and Jimmy again."

Her husband looked up at her, disgusted. "I say Maggie's no daughter of mine iffen she's fool enough to welcome him home. And don't ye go sneakin' on up to see her!"

Susannah crossed over to her loom and picked up an armload of fresh-spun wool. She carried the skeins to the boiling pot and dropped them into the yellow-brown dye, stirring them with a long stick.

"I'll heed ye for a time, Henry Wilkinson, for I don't wish to meddle in the young folks' business," she muttered through the pipe in her teeth. "But there ain't a man in this county or the next who can keep womenfolk apart when they need each other."

Henry looked at me, rolling his eyes, then spat onto his boot. "Womenfolk! Bah!" He rubbed ashes into the spit until the old leather shined like new.

As the days passed I followed my chores like always, keeping one eye on Clem as I worked. He tramped over his fields on long, slow legs, Calhoun following at his heels. Here and there he stopped to look around at the hills, or to kneel and sift a handful of earth through his fingers.

Eliza came to me one day in the barn where I was mucking out Sally's stall. "When're we movin' on, Jacob?" she asked. "On up to Iowa, like you said we would?"

"Come spring," I answered.

"It's spring now."

"No it ain't. It'll get cold again. You wait and see."

She peered out the barn door at the wandering man in the fields. "I don't like it here since he came. Why can't we go now?"

I stopped work and leaned on the pitchfork. "Because I got some business to attend to first."

"What business?" she asked.

I crossed over to the barn door and pulled it almost shut till we stood in the dark with one streak of sunlight squeezing in through the crack. "I'm gonna take care of that bushwhacker," I whispered.

"How?"

"Never you mind. Just keep quiet, and wait. When I've done what I set out to do...that's when we'll head north."

"Jacob, you leave that tomahawk be!" Eliza flew wild-eyed toward me and grabbed fistfuls of my shirt. "God sees everything, Jacob. You wouldn't dare do murder."

I peeled her hands off me and went back to shoveling straw. "I ain't gonna lay a hand on Clem," I said. "Now go on back to the house."

Eliza stood quiet, twisting one of her braids around her finger. I could tell she was trying to figure me out. Finally she spoke up. "Jacob?"

"What now?"

"You won't let Maggie get hurt, will you? Don't you think she's been almost as good as a ma to us?"

"Yes, Eliza. Now go on up to the house. Get back to your spring cleanin'." She backed slowly toward the barn door, pushed it open, and ran off.

It wasn't but a few hours till the chance I'd hoped for came along. After supper, as Jimmy lay asleep in his cradle near the hearth, Maggie and Eliza mended in the rockers while I sat cross-legged on the rug, whittling.

Clem rested in the horsehair chair, his boots stretched out toward the fire. Though he seemed to sleep, he was wide awake, his dull eyes fixed on the flames. His fingers pulled at one of the handlebars of his mustache awhile, then made their way to his belt and found the bowie knife he wore. He pulled it out and turned it over and over, running his fingers back and forth along the side of the shiny steel blade. The long, rough fingers and the cold, smooth blade clung together like cuddling sweethearts, and as I watched Clem out the corner of my eye I felt a chill go up my spine. I guess Maggie felt uneasy too. She set her sewing down.

"You surely do need new boots, Clem!" she declared. "Why, these old ones ain't much better than those you came home in, what with the seams splittin' like that. Whyn't you go into Linneus and order some?"

"Can't," he answered, his eyes stuck on the burning logs. "Joel says I'd best stay home awhile. Till tempers cool."

I kept up my wood carving, nice and easy, but my heart pounded in my ears, beating the inside of my chest like a hammer. "I'll go," I said. "I'll ride Lazarus in tomorrow."

"Would you, Jacob? Oh, I'd be so obliged," said Maggie, turning thankful eyes on me.

I shifted in my seat, dropping my eyes into my lap. When I spoke next I tried to look back up at her, but couldn't. "I'll take one of Clem's boots to be measured." I whittled on, trying to steady my breath and let my heart's wild gallop slow down to the steady rhythm of the mantel clock. "I'll say it's for Henry."

Maggie was thoughtful. "Yes." She nodded. "That'd be best. Likely no one in town but Joel even knows Clem's home. We'd best keep it that way."

Clem turned to Maggie. "Yer pa ain't been up to the house."

"No," she said, "I expect he'll come when he's ready."

Clem returned his knife to his belt and twitched one side of his mustache up in a half smile. "I reckon it's just as well."

Early next morning I saddled up Lazarus and rode into Linneus. I waited my turn at Metzger's, holding Clem's worn-out boot under one arm. The boot maker glanced up at me as he fit shoes on another customer, so I winked to let him know I'd come for more than new boots. He raised his eyebrows and broke into a big smile. When the customer had gone, Metzger held up Clem's ragged boot in the window's light, turning it from side to side.

"Seems a shame to spend the money, don't it, Jacob?" he chuckled. "These old boots would have lasted that Rebel the rest of his life!"

The Circuit Rider

Riding home bareheaded beneath the February sun, I thanked God I hadn't fled Missouri before I'd had the chance to avenge my family. Though I couldn't touch the stinking cowards who'd burnt our home and run us off our land, the Almighty had delivered Clem Canaday right into my hands. Any fool could see he was one of their kind. The way I saw it, in striking Clem down I'd have a hand in punishing them too.

My chest fairly burst with satisfaction at the thought of the deal I'd struck with Metzger and Wheeler. It was no deal, really—when the boot maker had opened his money box to pay me off, I'd refused to take any. All I wanted was to see justice done, I'd insisted. If the sheriff and the provost marshal wouldn't give a burning, thieving, Rebel bushwhacker what he deserved, Jacob Knight would. I was eager to see him pay for what his kind had done to me.

If there'd been any doubt in my mind that I'd done the right thing, walking a second time through the refugee camp wiped it away. Again, there'd been no sign, no word of my family. Seeing all those homeless folk made me sick inside. Someone ought to see to it that at least one bushwhacker paid for his crimes, and that someone might as well be me. The secret revenge felt soft against my mind, like clover on bare toes in summertime; it smelled sweet, like honeysuckle, and I breathed it in deep, along with the smell of the warming hills and their long-buried grasses.

As for Maggie, she'd probably fall down on her knees and thank me one day when she realized I'd saved her from being arrested and punished for sheltering a bushwhacker.

Furthermore, I'd caught sight of a newspaper in Linneus. That fellow named Grant had captured two Confederate forts back in Henry's old home, Tennessee. The Rebel generals had run off like cowards, and the Yankees had gone on to take Nashville. I could hardly contain my joy at the thought of telling Henry all about it. Yes sir, it wouldn't be long now before the Rebels got whipped for good!

After breakfast next morning Clem strolled out to the barn and took the long-handled scythe off its hook on the wall. Through the kitchen window Maggie watched him haul it toward a patch of prairie grass run wild over a section of fallow field.

"Jacob, go and help Clem," she said. "He looks so tired."

Grabbing up another griddle cake, I rolled it up and stuffed it in my mouth before going for my coat. Then I followed Clem to where he stood, pulling the whetstone out of his coat pocket. Barely glancing over at me, he leaned the scythe's shaft across the back of his left shoulder, holding on tight to the blade's dull edge. Then he spit on the stone in his right hand and with it took long, smooth strokes along the blade's cutting edge. He closed his eyes, swaying gently with the rhythm of the sharpening, and he made me think of old Henry playing his fiddle.

Satisfied the blade was ready, Clem pocketed the whetstone and wrapped his hands around the scythe's handles. He leaned his lanky frame forward, rocking it from side to side in a slow, steady swing through the grass. The thick, high grass fell easy prey to the sharp blade, and when he'd mowed the length of the patch he came back and held the scythe out to me.

Back home, my pa'd been the one to handle the scythe. When I took hold of its handles, I felt clumsy, like I was trying to dance with a partner twice my size. I bent over like I'd seen Clem do and tried to mow, but before long my arms and back ached enough to make me stop.

Clem stood watching with his arms crossed. "Don't just swing yer arms. Swing yer whole body," he advised.

I closed my eyes, trying to remember what I'd seen him do, keeping right at it until that scythe seemed to become a part of me, and the mowing came easy. Clem wandered back to the barn and left me to my work. Sweat ran down my neck and back but I mowed on, not wanting to break the steady rhythm. By the time Clem returned with Lazarus and the wagon, my shirt was soaked beneath my coat.

We pitched the cut grass till the wagon was full. When Clem tossed his pitchfork onto the wagon and struck out toward the field's far edge, I followed him. He stopped at a split rail fence that divided his land from another man's, then turned and leaned his back against the rails, crossing his arms and looking out over his own fields.

"Come April," he said, pointing at a field of dead corn stubble, "I'll plow all that up and plant me some wheat. Been corn there four years runnin', and it's just about sucked all the life out of that ground."

"Yes sir," I replied, leaning my hands on the oak rail, facing in the opposite direction. The wood had soaked up the sunshine and felt warm on my palms. I strained my eyes as far north as I could, wondering if the same clouds shifting across the blue sky on the horizon could be seen from Aunt Lucille's place up in Iowa.

We stayed like that a long time, him staring off one way, me another. When he finally spoke I fairly jumped, I'd been so deep in thought.

"That's a right pretty horse you've got yourself," Clem said, pulling his bowie knife from his belt. Turning it over and over in his hands, he gently fingered the horn handle and the two-edged blade without looking down at the knife. He gazed out across his fields like he had no idea what his hands were up to. But I couldn't take my eyes off that weapon.

The twirling blade caught the sunlight and shined it straight into my eye. A shiver ran from the back of my neck down to my heels at the thought that this horse thief had his eye on my Sally. Oath or no oath, Clem didn't fool me. His hands spoke true, cuddling up to his knife every chance they got, fingering the barrel of his Navy pistol of an evening as he sat beside the fire. Clem had a Rebel's heart, bent on making trouble, and having to lie low on his farm while the war burnt its tracks all over Missouri was like to kill him.

Clem startled all of a sudden, looking down at me. My face went hot when I realized I'd been gawking at him. He stared at the knife in his hand as if laying eyes on it for the first time, then slipped it back into its leather sheath.

"Maggie says you got bushwhacked," he said.

My throat went dry, and I wrapped my arm around the fence rail to hold myself up, suddenly feeling as if my knees would buckle. "Yes sir," I replied, almost choking. "We were burnt off our land."

Clem said nothing, just nodded and then picked some dirt out of one of his fingernails. I tried to walk away but my legs wouldn't hold me, and I felt dizzy. Blood pounded harder and harder in my head and something inside me wanted to get out. I struggled to hold it in, not knowing what to do, until finally it burst out without any help from me.

"The dirty bushwhackin' cowards!" I cried. "They had no right!"

Clem stopped picking at his fingernail and looked up at me. His eyes were hard and cold and squinted up, but I met them anyway, and held them in my own stare. I lay a hand on the tomahawk hanging from my belt, feeling the strength coming back into my legs. There was nothing this bushwhacker could do to me that I couldn't do to him first. Somewhere deep inside I'd crossed a line, and for the first time since he'd come home I knew I wasn't afraid of him.

I drew a deep breath and steadied myself against his gaze. But then he surprised me. Little by little his eyes softened up, till he finally took them off mine and looked away out over my shoulder at nothing in particular.

"Maybe they had no right," he drawled softly. "But I'll reckon they had their reasons."

"Reasons!" I spat, outraged. "There's no reason in this world good enough to burn decent folk off their farms. You got to know one thing about me, Clem," I said, my voice atremble with anger. "I'm a Union man, and always will be."

Clem looked me in the face again, and I saw his brown eyes shine wet. "So ye're loyal to the Union, boy. Well, just pray to the good Lord they don't kill yer loyalty the way they kilt mine."

He went back to staring out over his fields, and I let go of the breath I'd been holding. My balled-up fists uncurled and I slid down against the fence post and squatted there on the ground, feeling worn-out inside. I wondered who "they" were. Why on earth did Clem turn Rebel?

When he finally spoke again he changed the subject. "Why ain't you in school? We got us one out on Linneus road."

"School teacher ran off," I answered, "and joined the Union army."

Clem eased himself down onto the middle fence rail, hooking his arms around the top one. "Maggie did all her schoolin' out there. So did I, what little I had."

I could hardly picture Clem sitting behind a school desk. "You did?"

"Only 'bout a month or two. When I had enough, I left."

"Just plain left?"

"Walked home one day at noontime. See, Jacob, I started late. I was a big old boy, learnin' to read right along with the little ones. The other big boys got after me somethin' terrible about that, till I felt so ashamed I didn't care if I ever learned to read. I found my pa in the field and told him I'd pretty near learned all I wanted to down at that schoolhouse."

"Did he whip you?" I asked, recalling what my pa'd most likely do in such a case.

Clem smiled and shook his head. "Naw, Jacob. He let go the plow, then took hold of my two hands and set them on the handles. He said, 'Clement Canaday, if ye're bound and determined yer book learnin's done, then from now on this farm is yer slate and this plow is yer pencil. Now you write yer lessons in the earth, boy,' he said. 'Write you a book in this ground you can leave to yer children and grandchildren to read, and I'll be proud enough of you.' Then he slapped the mule's rump and I took off behind that plow. And as I went I thanked God for a pa like him. I've loved this farm somethin' fierce ever since that day."

Just then a rustling sounded behind us. We both wheeled around to see Maggie and Eliza come picking their way across the field, carrying Jimmy and a basket of fresh, hot corn pones. Clem reached out and took his son, tossing him high in the air and catching him. Then he sat him gurgling and kicking on the fence rail and held him there with one arm.

"Looky there, boy!" said the outlaw, sweeping his free arm wide across the fields. "Yer daddy's gonna write you a book. Just look out acrost those pages! Yes sir, one day you'll read it to yer grandbabies."

Maggie came alongside me. She put her arm around my shoulder and gave it a little squeeze, her face looking like sunshine beneath the shade of her bonnet. I'd never seen it look like that. When Eliza passed out the steaming hot corn cakes I grabbed up two, but to my surprise I could hardly get them down. Though the sun said noontime, I wasn't hungry. I watched Clem swinging his son around and talking about his family's future. The sweet cakes tasted sour in my mouth and I felt a gnawing in my gut all the rest of that day.

During the days that followed, clouds sank down onto the hills and stayed there. The white mist was so cold and thick, we all stayed inside and busied ourselves with whatever we could find to do. Clem sat cross-legged at the hearth, whittling sheep and pigs to keep Jimmy's oak horse company. Jimmy sat next to him, chawing and slobbering on the horse's head, and banging it hard on the floorboards. I watched them as I blackened Maggie's high-button shoes. Clem played with his little son the way my own pa had played with me when I was small; he looked at him all proud, the way a pa ought to look at his boy. Seeing Clem whittle toys for Jimmy gave me a warm feeling inside at first. But when I let my thoughts run on, my insides slowly turned cold. Because of Clem's bushwhacking kind, I had no more pa.

A few nights later, after Eliza'd pulled on her nightdress, she squatted down and reached deep between the bed tick and the ropes that held it up.

She pulled out some kind of cloth sack. She lit a second candle with the one already burning and scooted them both to the night table's edge. Then she climbed into bed and reached into the sack for a scrap of linen, some red thread, and a needle shining in the candles' light.

"What in—"

"Talk quiet, Jacob! This is secret. I don't want Clem knowin' about it."

"'Bout what?" I whispered. "Can't you do your stitchin' by the fire after supper instead of in bed at sleepin' time?"

She shook her head like I was trying her patience. "No, because then he'd see me. And he can't see it yet. His birthday's not till Sunday next."

I leaned over her shoulder as she unfolded the linen. It was shaped like a square and she'd finished off the edges. In the middle she'd sewn the words Our Father Which Art In Heaven, Hallered Be...

"Hallered's wrong," I pointed out. "It's *hallowed.*"

She snatched the handkerchief up close to her chest. "Never you mind! Just let me do my work, 'cause I've got lots more letters to stitch. I got this far when you and Clem were outside workin'. Maggie let me. Now Sunday's comin' quick and I've got to sew at night too."

"Eliza, this thing is for Clem?"

She nodded her head and tried to poke a thread through the needle. I stared at my sister, confused.

"Are you crazy?" I said, forgetting to whisper. "Weren't you just a few days ago beggin' me to get you out of here, away from that bushwhackin' Rebel outlaw? And now you're sewin' finery for him?"

She looked up at me with a blank face, almost like she'd forgotten Clem was our enemy. I wanted to slap sense into her; instead I yanked the cloth out of her hands and rolled out my side of the bed onto the floor.

"You better think again if you think you're going to give this to Clem!" I said, wadding the linen up in my fist and holding it high. "No Knight is goin' to give gifts to a bushwhacker as long as I live!"

"Jacob, hush your mouth!" Eliza stood up on the bed and jumped on top of me, her arms flailing toward the cloth. She knocked me off my balance and we both reeled backward, slamming against the wall. She straddled my waist and kicked my backside with her bare feet, all the while clutching and clawing at my hand that held the cloth. She'd got my hand in both of hers and was working at prying my fingers loose from her sewing when the door burst open and there stood Maggie.

"Eliza! Jacob! What the devil is goin' on here?" She folded her arms, waiting for an answer.

"Maggie, he—"

"Uh…I was just teasin' Eliza," I said, cutting my sister off. I looked at Eliza with a sad face. "I'm sorry." I turned back to Maggie and smiled.

"I swear, you almost woke the whole county!" she said. She closed the door, then opened it again to peek in. "Blow out the candle now. It's late."

When she'd gone I hurled Eliza's cloth across the room and she bolted after it.

"Now see what you did!" she snapped as she tried to smooth out the wrinkles in the cloth. "Now we have to put out the light."

I climbed in bed and glared at her. "You don't understand, Eliza, Clem is a bushwhacker. He burned down Asa Wheeler's farm—"

"No, you don't understand, Jacob," she butted in. "Are you blind? Don't you see it?" She kneeled on the bed and stuck her face in front of mine. "Maggie smiles now that Clem's home. She didn't do that before. Did she?"

I didn't answer.

"Did she, Jacob?"

"No," I whispered, then I rolled over to face the wall and pulled my pillow up around my ears, pretending to fall asleep in case she said anything more.

The warm spell had lasted so long the dogwoods began to show leaf. About that time a circuit rider came out from the east in a one-seated black buggy. He rode from farm to farm, inviting folk to a Sunday meeting in the Methodist church out on Morris Road. When he came to Maggie's door, her face lit all up at the thought of a Sunday meeting. I was pleased myself. We Knights had always been a churchgoing family, and I felt somehow that this would please my folks, wherever they were.

Come Sunday morning we got ready to leave the house all dressed up good and proper. Even Jimmy wore a new homespun coat his grandmammy had stitched for him and sent to Maggie by way of me. Clem hitched Lazarus up to the wagon and lent a hand to help us all in. But then he turned back toward the house.

"Ain't you comin', Clem?" Maggie looked surprised, for he'd taken his Saturday night bath just the same as the rest of us. "Folks around here might be more likely to forgive a church-goin' man."

He sat himself down on the front steps. "Naw," he said, leaning his elbows on his knees and turning his face up to the sun. "Joel says I got to stay home, and I don't know but what he ain't right."

Maggie hung her head. "I'm sorry. Sometimes I just wish things would go back to bein' the way they used to." She flapped the reins over Lazarus's rear end, and we took off.

The church out on Morris Road was a square, white building with a steeple and fancy pointed windows like our own church back home. Just behind it, three rows of wood and stone grave markers stretched up toward the hilltop.

Maggie's folks met us outside the church door. Henry offered Maggie a stiff hand to shake, but Susannah hugged her tight and gave her a smacking kiss on the forehead, then kissed Jimmy. The old captain looked mighty stiff and uncomfortable in his linen suit; he seemed almost naked without his tomahawk and shot pouch. He had his dogs, though, all six of them hanging close around his feet. Now and then he pulled small bits of jerky out of his suit pocket and held it down to them. They swiped their long wet tongues all over his greasy fingers and he wiped their slobber onto his pants legs. Neither he nor Susannah spoke one word about Clem's return.

Wagon after wagon pulled into the churchyard until a fair-sized crowd waited around the door. Across the way, Asa Wheeler stood talking to two fine-dressed ladies. He caught my eye between their fluttering bonnet strings and gave me a nod. I looked away, hoping no one had seen it. All of a sudden my Sunday clothes felt too warm; I tugged at my collar and fumbled with my jacket buttons, trying to loosen them. When the circuit rider's buggy turned up the church drive we all shuffled inside and took our seats.

I don't recollect what all we sang that morning, though we sang a good deal. I never did know that preacher's name, and I hardly remember him taking his place at the front of the church and beginning to speak. All my life I'd had a hard time keeping my mind from wandering out church windows of a Sunday morning, particularly a sunny one. Try as I might, my eyes just naturally fixed themselves on the changing pictures the little white clouds made as they floated across the sky.

The preacher's low, steady voice flowed like a quiet stream through the back of my brain while I sat still, seeing all kinds of cloud pictures. How long he ran on like that I don't know, but I'll never forget the sound of his Bible slamming up against the church wall.

My head jerked toward the front of the room just in time to see the preacher's Holy Book fall to the floor, its pages all aflutter. He'd heaved it there, his white-bearded face afire with rage. Then he turned fierce eagle eyes to us all.

"Where are the peacemakers?"

I could have heard a button drop in that church just then, and it seemed to me everyone sucked his breath in at the same time. I pressed myself hard against the back of my seat, waiting. But the old man wouldn't speak. He paced from one side of the church to the other, back and forth, back and forth, his hands clasped behind his back. After awhile I glanced from side to side, and others began to do the same.

The church door was open a crack, and a small group of slaves who'd driven their masters to church stood outside it, listening to the preaching. One of them pushed the squeaky door open wider and called out, "Go on preachin'! We're listenin'!"

*The preacher heaved his Bible against the church wall,
his white-bearded face afire with rage.*

The reverend halted in his tracks. He shut his eyes and dropped his chin to his chest like he was praying. After a minute or so he brought his head up again and opened his mouth to speak.

"I've been all up and down this state of Missouri," he began. "I've driven my buggy from St. Louis to Kansas City, from these northern hills to the Ozark mountains. Do you know what I've seen?"

We sat silent.

"Do you?"

We waited.

"Do you know what I've seen?" he thundered.

"No!" cried the slave from behind the church door.

The preacher began to pace again. "I've seen blood. I've seen murder. I've seen women and children, widows and orphans, fleeing for their very lives, chased by cowards with guns." The old man came to rest before the lectern. He grasped both sides of it, raising himself high onto his black-booted toes. "And my friends, I've seen Unionist and Secessionist alike take up arms and do evil to one another."

He walked over to where his big black Bible lay in a heap on the floor and stooped to pick it up. Then he slammed it down on the lectern and flipped angrily through the pages. "Now hear the Word of the Lord! 'Dearly beloved, avenge not yourselves, but rather give place unto wrath: for it is written, Vengeance is *mine!* I will repay, saith the Lord.' "

He paused, sweeping angry eyes across our faces. "Did you hear it, Missourians? *Did you hear it?*" he bellowed, and the walls and roof rattled from the thunder of his voice. Raising an arm, he pointed an accusing finger at us all. "*Shame* to Missouri.

Shame to her! For she ought to be an example to the rest of the nation of how brothers can live in peace, but instead she has become a symbol of wanton bloodshed! Missouri has given herself over to the satisfying of her vengeful desires, and woe to her! For the wrath of God is being poured out upon her!"

He hovered over his Bible again, reading farther down the page, this time in a voice so small I had to lean forward to hear it right. "Therefore if thine enemy hunger, feed him; if he thirst, give him drink.... Be not overcome of evil, but overcome evil with good."

The reverend slammed his Bible shut. Flecks of dust whirled upward from it into the sunlight streaming across the lectern from the east window. Feeling like I'd had the wind knocked out of me, I leaned forward in my seat, gripping the front edge of the pew seat till my knuckles turned white.

Now his voice sank to a whisper, but the whisper screamed in my ears and shot through the room, "Blessed are the peacemakers, for they shall be called the children of God."

He took his seat. The song leader half stood, confused, looking around the room. We all sat as still as stones, afraid to move or speak.

Three rows ahead of me, a man stood up so fast his hymn book flopped to the ground. Pushing his way past the others in his pew, he stomped clench-fisted down the aisle toward the door. It was Asa Wheeler, his eyes ablaze, his mouth curled down in an angry scowl. A lady I guessed must be Mrs. Wheeler stood and followed him, her swishing skirts the only sound in the room. Four children followed her. When the last one out had slammed the door, the song leader scared up his courage and stood to lead us in a closing hymn.

Come, ye sinners, poor and needy,
Weak and wounded, sick and sore;
Jesus ready stands to save you,
Full of pity, love, and power.

I stared out the window at some swaying willow branches the whole time we were singing. My own ma had recited that very same Bible verse to me when I was small, on the day I'd kicked another child in Boonesboro for grabbing away my peppermint stick. "…Vengeance is mine, saith the Lord." It struck me now that my folks might not agree with the way I'd taken—mixing in with Asa Wheeler's revenge.

Let not conscience make you linger,
Nor of fitness fondly dream;
All the fitness He requireth,
Is to feel your need of Him.

Feeling dizzy, I held tight to the pew back in front of me. I bent over a minute to catch my breath, then brought myself up straight again when Maggie set her hand on my shoulder.

Come, ye weary, heavy laden,
Lost and ruined by the fall;
If you tarry till you're better,
You will never come at all.

Well, Asa's revenge was my revenge too. Already I'd waited too long. And I'd been choosing my own path without my folks' say-so for nigh four months.

That afternoon I kept to myself, mostly. I wandered down to the creek woods, slinging my tomahawk at tree trunks, practicing my aim. I tried to think, but the preacher's bellowing voice bounced around in my head. Sure, it was easy enough for a white-headed preacher to ride around the countryside and tell other folks to forgive. But most likely he'd never been bushwhacked. What did he know about coming home to find his house burnt down, his family gone? Still, that preacher's words, "...Vengeance is mine, saith the Lord," kept coming back to me, sometimes in his own voice, sometimes in Joel's, and sometimes in my ma's. They spoke so clear, it almost seemed like any minute they'd jump out from behind a hickory tree. Twice I looked around to make sure I was really alone in the woods.

I walked along the banks of the Locust, stopping at Clem's old fire pit, now long cold. Standing there, kicking the ashes around with the toe of my boot, I heard a sudden commotion on the opposite bank of the creek.

A gang of crows was pestering a hoot owl in a tree. The sun dipped low, it being just that time of day when the owls wake up and the crows go to roost. I guess those bullying birds wanted some sport before bedtime, judging from the way they went after that owl. They flung themselves straight at him, pretending to attack, then changed direction at the last minute, to confuse him. Coming at him from all sides, they laughed at him with screeching caws, circled around, and dove at him again and again. With each attack, the sorely outnumbered owl ducked his head and flapped his wings.

I felt my anger rise until my fingers gripped hard around the handle of my tomahawk. "You all git!" I shouted, running to the water's edge and flinging the war hatchet as hard as I could right at where the crows were thickest. The spinning steel blade just missed one, but the handle hit another bird hard, knocking him to the ground, sending the rest of his gang flapping up into the sky and away over the fields. The owl flew off in the opposite direction, gliding low over my head. By the time I'd run upstream and crossed over the creek on a log stretched from bank to bank, the crow I'd hit had got back to his feet. As I ran toward my tomahawk, I saw him lift off, kind of dazed and crooked, to follow his friends. Feeling mighty satisfied with myself, I stuck the hatchet in my belt and struck out for home.

Coming around the hawthorns up near the house, I heard my name called out. Down the dusky drive limped Henry for the first time since Clem's return. His fiddle was strapped to his back, and Susannah followed right behind him.

The smell of hot bacon grease and frying fritters hit us full in the face as we walked in the door. Crouched beside the spider pan, Maggie broke into a big smile when she looked up and saw her folks had come. Clem stood stiff and still as a frozen corn stalk, but Susannah rushed straight to him, not even bothering to take off her wraps. Reaching up and pinching his chin between her gnarled fingers, she smiled up into his face.

"Well, ye've come back to us, Clem," she said. "That's good, real good. I knowed ye weren't a Rebel deep down!"

Clem pressed his lips together hard, staring down at his feet. He put his big hand over both Susannah's and gave them an awkward pat.

Henry stomped over to him then, nudging his wife aside. The old man cleared his throat two or three times. "We was fixin' to give ye up fer dead," he mumbled. "Now ye're back, and only God knows why they let ye off without a hangin'. Well, Clement, I'm glad ye're back...for Maggie's sake." The captain stuck out a stiff hand, and Clem shook it.

Then Henry reached inside his buckskin shirt and pulled out something long and thin. I moved up close to see. It was a pipe, carved of stone, with woven porcupine quills all along its wooden stem. White feathers dangled from it, fastened on with leather strips.

"Ye know what white feathers mean, don't ye, Clem?" asked Henry.

Clem shook his head. "Ye're the squaw man, Henry. You tell me."

"Peace!"

The bushwhacker smiled. He reached out and took hold of the pipe, then squatted down to examine it closer to the fire's light. Henry dropped down and sat cross-legged beside him.

"Quick, Jacob, light a match," whispered Maggie.

I lit a match in the fire, then handed it to Henry. He held it to the bowl, sucking long and deep, then handed it to Clem through a sweet, smoky cloud.

Clem looked a mite confused by all the reconciling, but I wasn't surprised by it one bit. I'd sneaked a look at Henry's face in church that morning, seen his forehead all puckered up and his mouth hanging open while the preacher hollered. I guessed the reverend's words had stuck themselves into Henry's brain like they had in mine, making him feel like he was sitting on a smoldering fire pit, and him knowing he'd have no peace till he jumped off of it and made things right. Still, Henry looked mighty uncomfortable in Clem's presence, as if it sapped all his inmost strength just to act civil.

We all sat down at table together and dipped our fritters in molasses. When the fritters were gone, Maggie sent Eliza down cellar to fetch a dried gooseberry pie she'd baked the day before. When we'd finished that off too, Henry tuned his fiddle while my sister and I pushed the rockers and the horsehair chair aside to the corners of the room. If houses could bust for joy, Maggie's might have done so that night, for once again Susannah clogged in the middle of the floor while Henry played as many Tennessee tunes as he could recall. Her bouncing shadow half covered Clem, who sat dandling Jimmy on his knee, keeping time with the heel and toe of his boot.

I once did have a big white horse,
Corn to feed him on;
Stay at home my pretty little miss,
And feed him when I'm gone.

When I was a little bitty boy,
All I wanted was a knife;
Now I am a great big boy,
And all I want is a wife.

Shady Grove, my true love,
Shady Grove I say,
Shady Grove, my true love,
I'm a-goin' away.

When Susannah grew tired, she plopped herself down in the rocker and lit her pipe. Henry fiddled on. As he broke into a reel, Maggie danced over and pulled me up off of my seat, laughing. She hooked her arm in mine and we spun around the room, first in one direction, then the other. Clapping hands and Eliza's laughing face whirled past until my stomach spun and my cheeks grew sore from laughing. Begging to be let off, I rolled onto the rag rug, sweating and trying to catch my runaway breath.

Not being tired out yet, Maggie ran over and grabbed up Jimmy from Clem's lap. Setting him on her hip, she took his fat little hand in hers and danced him around nice and slow in the circle of firelight. Henry slowed his fiddling down to Maggie's feet, but after a spell she finally tired out and sat down with her baby.

That's when Clem stood up. His boots clomped across the floor till he stood in front of Eliza. He held out his hands to her. She bit her lip and scrunched her head down between her shoulders, staring into her lap, but he stayed put. Finally he grabbed her by the hands and pulled her out of the shadows into the middle of the room. Around and around in the firelight they twirled, Clem sometimes picking up his little partner and spinning her around until she burst into a loud, dizzy laugh. When the fiddling stopped, Clem bowed to Eliza and she curtsied back to him, covering her face with her hands and giggling.

While Maggie served us all cider, Eliza slipped upstairs and came down again with a little gift wrapped in a scrap of calico. We all hushed as she made her way over to Clem and handed it to him.

"Maggie says today's your birthday," she mumbled, blushing pink.

Clem took the gift from her hand and stepped over to the hearth. There he pulled off the calico wrapping and unfolded the handkerchief. Tilting it down toward the fire's light to see it better, he labored over the words with his forehead all wrinkled up.

At least he won't know hallowed's spelled wrong, I thought to myself, remembering what he'd said about leaving school before he'd all the way learned to read.

Clem looked at Eliza. "You done this all by yerself?"

Eliza smiled and twisted fistfuls of her apron in her hands. "Yes sir. It's only part of the Lord's Prayer 'cause I couldn't finish in time."

"I reckon half a prayer's better than none," Clem said, his mustache twitching like it always did when he half smiled. "It's real fine. I'll be proud to carry it in my pocket." He strolled back to his chair and sat down, spreading the handkerchief out on his knee to admire it.

Henry drained his second cup of cider dry and smacked his lips, his scarred, leathery skin glowing orange in the crackling firelight. "Had news from a traveler today," he said after wiping his mouth with his shirtsleeve.

"What news, Pa?" Maggie asked.

Henry turned to Clem. "News of General Price and his men."

"Old Pap?" Clem looked up from admiring his birthday gift.

"Yer 'Old Pap' hightailed it out of Missouri nigh upon one week ago!" announced Henry with satisfaction. "General Sam Curtis chased him clean out of Springfield. Yes sir, the Yankees run him right down into Arkansas!"

Clem sat dumbfounded. He whispered, "Where's McCulloch?"

I knew Ben McCulloch was another general the Missouri Secesh had pinned their hopes on. He'd fought alongside Price at Wilson's Creek and helped him beat back the Yankees.

"Don't know!" declared Henry. "Seems he ought to have helped that old whiskey-drinkin' Price out, but he never showed up!" The old man hooted and slapped his knee. "Missouri belongs fair and square to the Yankees now. And I say God preserve the Union!"

Clem bolted to his feet, his new handkerchief floating to the floor. "I ain't gonna listen to this in my own house!"

"Pa!" scolded Maggie, rising from her rocker with a sleeping Jimmy in her arms. She planted herself in the middle of the room, between her husband and father.

Hoisting himself to his feet, Henry limped straight to her, glaring at Clem over her shoulder. "If that husband of yers had a lick of courage he'd join up with Price's men and do his fightin' on the battlefield, 'stead of bushwhacking by night!" The old man's face twitched with fury as his hand found the war hatchet hanging from his belt. "Why, iffen I was young again, I'd—"

"Well, ye ain't!" put in Susannah.

Henry's mouth snapped shut.

"You all hush!" Maggie cried.

Clem turned without another word and stalked out the front door, slamming it behind him. Eliza ran to where the handkerchief lay and snatched it up. She bolted to the front door and flung it wide.

"Clem! Clem, you forgot what I stitched for you! Come back here! Come on back and get your present!"

Outside, the wind whistled through the branches of the walnut tree and across the bare fields. Clem didn't answer. Eliza turned and marched inside, kicking the door shut behind her. She shot Henry a fierce look.

"Now look what you did! Why'd you bother to bring that old peace pipe of yours anyway?" She ran upstairs crying, the handkerchief balled up in her fist.

Not two seconds after she'd gone, a sudden shower of sparks burst out of a burning log, shooting across the brick hearth and onto the floor. Quick as lightning, Susannah jumped up and grabbed the hearth broom. She rounded them up, pushing them back into the fireplace.

"Man's born to trouble as sure as sparks fly upward," she muttered as she swept, wagging her head and clucking her tongue. "That's what the Old Book says. And this war's brought a heap of it on our family!"

"I know Clem's made more than his share of trouble," added Maggie sadly. "But it's time to just let him be. Do it for me, Pa."

Henry looked just about as sorry then as I'd ever seen a man look. He ran both his hands through his wild white hair as if trying to rub sense into his brain. "And me wantin' to patch things up tonight like the preacher said!" he moaned, hanging his head. "I'm a heap sorry, Maggie! My Union feelings ran high, that's all. I'll make amends, child. I give ye my word I will."

Susannah snatched the pipe from her lips. "Sit down, old man, and pick up yer fiddle. Ye've gabbled enough for one night!"

Meekly, Henry obeyed his wife. As if to smooth things over with Clem through his music, he played "O Listen to the Mockingbird," a song everyone in Missouri knew was a favorite of Secesh folk.

~

The following morning Clem drifted through the house from window to window, tapping his fingers on the panes and gazing out over his fields. A little before noon he hitched Lazarus to the plow, but dug only half a furrow before coming back inside.

"It ain't no use," he muttered, tossing his hat down on the kitchen table. He dropped into a chair and lay his forehead in his hands till Maggie set his dinner in front of him. He'd only half finished when he pushed his salt pork and cabbage away and began to drum his fingernails on the tabletop.

"Clem, why'n't you and Jacob go outside and chop some wood?" suggested Maggie, tying her apron behind her back. "The woodbox is near empty, and fresh air'll do you good." She smiled and even laughed a little, but as I trailed Clem out to the woodpile I turned back and saw her in the kitchen window, watching us. Her smile had gone.

That afternoon a freezing wind blew down from the north; by evening a light snow dust covered the hills. While Maggie and Eliza got supper, Clem sat by the fire with Jimmy on his knee. He didn't speak. All evening long he sat just staring, now and then pulling out his knife like he always did. Not one of us spoke to him; something in his face told us not to. Dark and hollow, his eyes seemed to have sunk even deeper into his head, and his fingers trembled as they caressed the knife.

The evening fire burned low. Like he did most nights, Calhoun went sniffing for crumbs he'd missed underneath the supper table. When his tail knocked against a chair and scooted it an inch or two across the floor with a loud scrape, Clem fairly flew from his seat and backed up to the fire. Holding out his knife to defend himself, his eyes darted wildly from the front door to the kitchen door. Eliza, darning socks in the rocker, screamed and pulled her apron up over her face.

Maggie threw aside her needlework. She rushed to Clem's side. She grabbed away his knife, tossed it onto the hearth, and shook him till his eyes lost that glazed look. "You're tired, Clem. Now you just come with me. The children can bank the fire tonight." She took hold of his trembling arm and led him toward the dark stairway. Meek as a frightened child, he followed her up to his room.

Long after Eliza fell asleep beside me that night, my eyes wouldn't shut. One week had passed by since I'd told the boot-maker of Clem's return. I thought of how worried Maggie was about Clem, how hard she was trying to keep his mind on the farm and his new life. Once again, I wondered if I'd done right in striking that deal with Metzger and Asa Wheeler.

But then again, what did Clem Canaday matter to me? Soon I'd be going on up to Iowa. I'd leave him and every other Missouri bushwhacker behind forever. Let Asa Wheeler and the boot maker watch him hang. After all, it was Asa's house he'd torched, not mine. I tried to feel the familiar sharp slicing of hate, but the blade within me felt dull. And when I slid my hand beneath my pillow toward the tomahawk, I almost didn't care that I didn't find it. For the first time since Henry'd given it to me I'd left it downstairs somewhere, and hadn't even missed it. I waited for sleep, prayed for it even, but it wouldn't come. I rolled from side to side on the lumpy cornhusks till Eliza woke and told me to stop.

Somewhere between midnight and sunup I finally dozed off. Whether I slept just fifteen minutes or three hours I don't know, but I do recall opening my eyes suddenly, staring into the dark. Thinking I'd heard something, I raised my head off the pillow. Yes, Calhoun had barked; he was doing it again. Thinking it was probably just another coon, I lay my head back down. Eliza mumbled in her sleep and turned over. The dog hushed. My eyes fell closed, but a horse's whinny and the jingling of spurs in the yard below yanked them open again. No sooner had I swung my bare feet to the floor than a wood-splintering crash shook the house.

Calhoun barked again, and Eliza shot up in the bed. "What's that, Jacob? Bushwhackers?"

"No," I mumbled.

A sinking feeling crawled into my gut. I ran to the bedroom door and flung it open. A blast of cold night air blew up the stairs and up under my nightshirt, raising gooseflesh on my bare legs. Gripping the door frame so hard my fingers hurt, I felt like my heart froze in my chest. Half a dozen masked men were climbing the stairway. I knew they were coming for Clem.

The first one carried a lantern in one hand and a pistol in the other. When he reached the top of the stairs, he held the light up to my face. I stepped back and shielded my eyes.

"Stand back, boy!" he growled, giving me a shove with one elbow. I stumbled backward a step or two, but shot right back into the doorway.

"Wait!" I hollered, but my voice went unheard beneath the clatter of boots on the wooden stairs. Someone kicked Clem and Maggie's door open with a crash. Maggie screamed, and Jimmy set to howling so that my breath caught in my throat. Jerusha had cried like that one night last October.

"Stop!" I lunged forward, clutching at the arm of the man who'd kicked the door, but as I did, two more men topped the stairs. One grabbed me from behind. The lantern's orange glare blinded me as he spun me around and shoved me headlong down the cold, dark stairway. My bones banged against the hard wood all the way down, till my face ground into the floor and my teeth sank deep into my bottom lip. With a spinning head I lay where I fell, too stunned to get up.

Not far away, Calhoun yapped and howled, and slowly I realized there were men on the front porch. The light of a burning torch shone through the splintered door, swinging back and forth on its hinges. Someone was wrestling with Calhoun, cursing angrily as he struggled to tie him up.

I sat up. A sharp pain shot through my head. I tasted blood in my mouth and heard boots thundering on the stairs above me. In the flickering light I saw two men half-carrying, half-dragging Clem down in his white nightshirt. Though his hands and feet were trussed up, Clem struggled and kicked till they dumped him on the floor not five feet from where I sat.

"You made a mistake sneaking back home, Clem Canaday,"

smirked the man with the lantern and the gun, setting his boot on Clem's chest. Right away I knew Asa Wheeler's voice. "We don't want no Rebel bushwhackers around here and we aim to make an example of you to anyone else of your kind."

"He took the oath!" I croaked. "You ask Joel Wilkinson, the sheriff!"

Asa held up his lantern to see me better. "Turned your back on us, ain't you, boy? Well, oath or no oath, Clem Canaday's gonna pay for what he done."

Two men flipped Clem over onto his stomach and held him in place by planting their boots on his back. Maggie shrieked from the top of the stairs as someone pushed her down ahead of him, twisting her arm behind her back.

"Leave my wife and kids be," begged Clem. "Just take me and be done with it!"

Asa chuckled behind his mask as the other men gagged Clem with a kerchief. "Poor little you, Clem. Why, this ain't no different than what you done to other folk all up and down Missouri. You burnt down my house and barn and run my wife and kids off the place, just for being good Union folk. Now it's your turn! The Yankees might give Rebel trash like you second chances, but we aim to see justice done."

A gunman pushed Maggie over Clem's bound body and she fell sprawling on the floor in her nightgown. I crawled to her, threw my arms around her, and hugged her tight.

Asa lifted the lantern high till its flickering light lit up her face. "Begging your pardon, ma'am, but you ought to have known better than to shelter a bushwhacker. Now gather all your children into your wagon and get on out of here, because this house is going to burn."

Hoot Owl's Call

Someone thumped in heavy boots toward where Clem lay, carrying a tar-smelling torch. The man's short, squat body and hairy wrists told me it was Metzger, though his face, like Asa's, was masked. Smoke curled up from the burning stick, crawling like a fat, gray snake across the ceiling and filling the room.

The boot maker laughed deep down in his throat. "Ja, Clem. Now you get what's coming to you."

Clem jerked to and fro, hollering behind his gag, but all he managed to do was roll himself a foot or two across the floor. Someone on the porch tossed Asa a coiled rope. He slung it over one shoulder. The strange, wild look in his eyes made my hair stand on end. I opened my mouth in protest, but before I could speak Maggie slapped her hands on my cheeks and jerked my face toward her.

"Jacob!"

I blinked my eyes. Ma! I could see her again, on the night we were burned out; I recognized the wild, frantic light in her eyes, the glare of the flames on her tear-streaked face. I lifted my hand to touch it, like I had so many times in my dreams since then. "Ma?" I whispered.

Maggie shook me so hard my teeth rattled. "Jacob! Run upstairs for Jimmy and Eliza! Wrap Jimmy up good. Now hurry!"

I did what I was told, though I fell flat on my face as soon as I stood up. With my head pounding, I struggled to my feet again. The gunmen at the foot of the stairs let me pass and I stumbled to the top.

Eliza sat in Maggie's bed, cradling Jimmy in her arms and singing to him in a soft, shaky voice. For the first time since I could remember I felt something close to respect for that girl. I knew she was afraid, yet there she was, thinking of someone else instead of herself.

"Get up!" I said. "We got to go!"

She looked up at me, her face as white as the moon. Without a word she shifted Jimmy to her shoulder and made to get out of the bed.

"Here!" I tossed her a blanket from the quilt rack near the door. "Wrap him up, quick. Follow me."

When we reached the bottom of the stairs, Asa waved his pistol at the door. "Go on, get!" he ordered. Turning to Maggie, who was still lying on the floor, he barked, "You too! Get in your wagon and go."

"She ain't even dressed!" I objected.

Asa stomped to a hook in the wall near the door, grabbed off Maggie's shawl, and flung it at her. With trembling hands she pulled it around herself as she got to her feet.

"Can't you find it in your heart to forgive, Asa?" she pleaded.

Asa snorted out a spiteful laugh, his eyes crinkling up above his kerchief mask. "The time for forgiving is over," he sneered, strutting over to Clem. He pressed the bottom of his boot on

Clem's belly and looked down on the man with contempt. "We, the Vigilance Committee, find you, Clement Canaday, guilty of bushwhacking for the Rebel Cause, and we aim to administer justice!" Turning to Maggie, he nodded his head toward the door. "Now get on out, Mrs. Canaday!"

With one last look at Clem, Maggie put her arm around Eliza and made for the door. Through the smoky haze from Metzger's torch, my eye caught hold of something shiny on the mantel. My tomahawk! It lay where I'd left it the night before when I'd come in with Henry and Susannah. Hoping no one had seen me look that way, I hung my head and followed Maggie outside.

It struck me as a mighty strange kindness coming from a murdering mob, but someone had managed to hitch Lazarus up to the wagon for us. Maggie hurried toward it with Eliza right behind her, but I lingered on the porch. Across the yard, I saw a masked man leading Sally out of the barn, and the truth hit me like a sharp kick in the gut. This horse-thieving mob was no different from the bushwhackers that'd run us off our place last fall back in Howard County. It just went by a different name, fought for another side in the war.

Calhoun had been tied to the porch rail with a rawhide whip. He strained and yanked at it, whining and yawling and looking up at me with wet, wild eyes. Asa Wheeler came up behind me, still toting his rope.

"Well, boy? Did you decide to stay and help us after all?"

When I turned to face him I saw clear for the first time since last October. In his eyes boiled my own angry spite, red-hot and raging; my own bitter gall drooled from his lips. Choking on my shame, I couldn't answer. He shrugged his shoulders and crossed the yard to the walnut tree. My bare legs shivered as I watched him toss the rope over a high branch and begin tying a noose at one end.

Two men burst out the door, fighting to keep hold of a struggling Clem. As they hauled him down the steps his eyes met mine, and in that moment I knew the truth about him too. The bushwhacker had a soul in him, just like me. My Maker had made him too, putting dreams in his head and feelings in his gut that made him act the way he did and think the way he thought. Sure, he didn't think or act in the way I would, nor fight on the same side of the war I'd choose to. And though he had no right to go bushwhacking, he had a right to live, like I had a right to.

Stuck to my spot with my teeth chattering, I heard a mighty flapping sound above my head. I looked up to see a dark shadow passing across the white night sky.

"Whoo whoo whoo whoo—ah! Whoo whoo whoo whoo—ah!"

A hoot owl glided over the snowy yard on his way to the creek woods. I watched his dark shadow till he disappeared into the dark western sky, wondering if he were the very same owl I'd freed down by the creek. Well, it hadn't taken much to scare off that band of crows, but what good was I against this murdering mob of men?

"Whoo whoo whoo whoo—ah!" came the far-off cry again. I stood frozen, my heart flapping like the great bird's wings. I breathed deep to steady myself. The rush of cold air seemed to lift me up high, so high I could see my way clear above the disaster at hand. All at once I knew the way I'd take, and the knowing made me strong.

"It's got to stop," I told myself, repeating what Joel Wilkinson had said on Christmas Day. "The bloodlettin' has to stop somewhere!" Just then I heard my name called out. Maggie had got Eliza and Jimmy into the wagon; now she was gripping the reins, ready to flee.

"Jacob, hurry!" shrieked Eliza. Maggie caught my eye and held it, silently urging me to join her. But I couldn't do it. My time had come.

I wheeled around and tore back into the house, straight for the mantel and my tomahawk. Grabbing it up, I turned to see Metzger through the smoky haze, standing near the window. He was holding his torch up to the curtains. The flame caught and began to crawl up, but I had no time for that now. With a screeching howl, I burst out the door and off the front porch. Waving my war hatchet high in the air, I rushed headlong toward Asa Wheeler as he bent over Clem to slip the noose around his head.

Asa heard me coming. He lifted his eyes, then jerked his whole body upright, dropping the rope. I let my hatchet go, spinning through the air, straight at him. The iron blade sunk into his shoulder. Roaring in pain, he staggered backward and clutched his wound, gaping at me wide-eyed. When he'd yanked the blade from his shoulder and hurled it across the yard, he made a move for the gun on his belt. Before he could touch it I shot my whole self into him. We rolled across the snowy ground, me tearing at his face with both hands and him trying to heave me off. My head slammed the ground so hard a shooting pain cut through it from back to front.

From somewhere beyond the spinning earth and sky I heard my name screamed out, but I stuck to Asa like a stinging bee. We tumbled all over creation, fighting for that gun. I pinned his shoulders to the ground but his hands found my neck and squeezed. Just as I knew I couldn't hold him anymore, he looked up past me and his eyes grew big. He loosened his grip and I rolled my eyes upward to see the muzzle of a flintlock rifle pointing right in Asa's face. Aiming it was a mighty black bear towering tall against the lightening sky.

"Ye're trespassin', Wheeler!"

"Henry!" I cried, breaking free of Asa and rolling away to one side. Henry's hounds ran pell-mell around the yard, cutting between men's legs and yapping as loud as they could. Over by the house, someone shouted and pulled out a gun, but before he could take aim, the ground began to shake. At the steady beat of oncoming horses, the men all stopped and looked around in a wild panic.

A string of riders, black against the snowy fields, thundered up the drive. As they rushed by me, lifting my hair with their speedy wind, my eye caught the shine of brass buttons beneath flapping overcoats. They circled the yard, rifles gleaming, and at their rear rode Joel Wilkinson, the sheriff.

"Yankees!" whooped Henry from beneath the bear's head, holding his rifle high and nearly dancing a jig. Near as I could count, at least thirty mounted Union soldiers circled the house and yard with guns pointed inward. Calhoun yanked so hard he finally snapped his leather tie, leaping off the porch and weaving through the horses' legs to where Clem lay trussed up beneath the walnut tree.

"Fire!" screamed Maggie, jumping to her feet in the wagon. Sure enough, the flames had taken hold of the curtains and the window frame, licking hot and red against the glass and sending smoke rolling out through the front door. An officer shouted something; five or six soldiers jumped off their mounts and ran right into the house. They tore off their overcoats and beat the flames with them, while we all began to gather up armfuls of snow to pile in a heap by the doorway. One by one the soldiers

Aiming the rifle was a mighty black bear towering tall against the lightening sky.

inside grabbed snow off the pile, and just when I thought we'd never keep up with them, the window went black and we knew the house was saved. We in the yard heard stomping and scuffling inside, and one shot fired. Before long Metzger and two more masked men filed out onto the porch with their hands held high, coughing and choking into their kerchief masks.

When Asa Wheeler caught sight of them, he pushed himself up off the snowy ground and staggered to his feet, still clutching his wound. He glared down at Clem, who lay beneath the swinging rope, forgotten in all the excitement. Calhoun stood between the two, baring his teeth at Asa.

The yard fell silent except for the jingling of spurs. Joel walked his horse into the middle of everything and turned in a slow circle.

"Clement Canaday's been pardoned by the provost marshal on account of he took the oath," he announced. "He ain't gonna be judged by farmers and boot makers!"

Asa stumbled into the center of the yard to face the sheriff. He flailed his unhurt arm around wildly in protest. "Damn the oath! Clem took it once already, then broke it. He burnt my home! He oughta pay for that. If you won't serve justice, the Vigilance Committee will!"

"Would you be guilty of the very same crime you accuse Clem of?" Joel asked him. "'Cause you ain't no better than Clem if you go burnin' down his house, Asa! And you're a heap worse than him if you do murder!"

"This ain't no surprise. The sheriff's Clem's kin!" Asa informed anyone who'd listen.

"Kin or no kin," answered Joel, "I say any man who takes the oath gets a chance to prove himself. Missouri's burnin' up like hell itself because of folk like you!" he cried. "Well, the fire's put out for now, at least on this farm. So go home!"

No one spoke. Sunup was coming on quick in the east, turning the snowy fields blood red in that direction. The horses stamped and snorted, and Calhoun let off a fretful howl.

"We don't want Rebel trash in this county!" shouted a masked man in the yard.

Joel wheeled his horse toward the speaker and pointed at Clem. "I'll say it again! Clem Canaday took the oath, and he aims to live true to it. Leave him be to do it!"

All eyes in the yard turned on the bushwhacker, whom Henry had loosed and ungagged. The old man pulled him to his feet and he stumbled toward the porch, ghostlike in his white nightclothes. Climbing the stairs on trembling legs, he looked up into the eyes of the men who'd come to kill him.

"Rest assured, I'll trouble this county no more," he said, then walked on past them and disappeared into the smoky house. Calhoun trotted after him.

Joel walked his horse right up to the porch. "I don't know who most of you are, and I don't want to know!" he shouted. "Now go home!"

Glaring up at the sheriff, the still-masked men filed past him toward where their horses were tethered, over behind the barn. One by one they mounted and slipped away across the hills, each in his own direction. Asa Wheeler went last of all, still clutching his wound. Joel begged him to wait, offering to bind it up for him with a torn-up cloth, but Asa wouldn't. He mounted his horse and turned around in the saddle.

"I'm on your side!" he informed the Yankees. "I ain't no Rebel lover like the sheriff here!"

"Then join the Army!" snickered a soldier and another one snorted out a laugh.

Asa wiped a bloody hand across his face and spat in the snow. "I don't back down easy." He spurred his horse and galloped away.

Joel helped his sister off the wagon, then lifted down Eliza and Jimmy.

"I thank you, Joel," whispered Maggie, pale and shaking. She looked around at all the Federal soldiers, fumbling at her nightdress and pulling it up tight across her neck. Seeming to want to speak, but not finding words, she finally reached down and took the baby from Eliza. Grabbing hold of Eliza's hand, she led her inside.

I lingered outside with Henry and his dogs to watch the soldiers ride away. The sun had sneaked up behind the clouds, washing the snowy hills with a thin, ragged light. Standing with one arm around the pillar post, my ears pounded with the drumming of the horses' hooves beating away up the drive. My chest felt full with satisfaction, like my heart had swelled up to twice its normal size.

"God save the Union!" Henry called after them, waving his rifle high.

"God save the Union!" I whispered.

The Soldier

Next morning, before even Jimmy woke up, I heard a creak on the front steps. Quietly I rose and pressed my forehead against the cold windowpane. There was Clem, walking down the drive toward the road, with his haversack and rifle slung over his shoulder.

Quickly I pulled on my pants and boots. I tiptoed down the stairs and across the kitchen to the back door, where Calhoun was whining softly to be let out. Grabbing my coat, I unlatched the door and set him free. I closed the door softly, then tore off after Clem, around the house and up the drive, nearly slipping in the snow as I ran.

When he heard me coming he stopped. Calhoun barked once; Clem grabbed his muzzle and shushed him. Clem turned around, half his face lit up by the rising sun, the other half in shadow. I slid to a stop. Beneath his open coat I saw the Navy pistol and bowie knife in his belt; his haversack bulged out with provisions from down cellar. I couldn't help gawking at it.

Clem looked from my face to his sack, then back at me. My throat began to ache, making me feel like I'd swallowed a stone the size of a goose egg.

"Where are you goin', Clem?"

He hesitated. "Down to Arkansas, to join me up with Old Pap's men."

His words cracked me on the jaw as clean as any fist. My mind reeled with the blow as my eyes smarted with hot tears.

"But you're saved now! Joel and the Yankees, Henry and me, we fought off a whole gang of murderers for you."

Clem shook his head, staring at his toes. I felt the blood rise hot into my neck and face.

"This is your chance, Clem. Ain't you goin' to take it?"

Clem bit his lower lip and scratched his nose. He put his hands on his hips and sighed, staring over my shoulder. "No, I ain't," he finally answered.

I wiped my eyes with a piece of my nightshirt hanging out below my coat sleeve. "You said you would! For Maggie."

Clem sucked in a couple of deep breaths. He turned away from me and took a few steps. Then he stopped and looked me in the eye.

"You've heard tell about me takin' the oath last summer, ain't you?"

I nodded.

"Well, I'm gonna tell you somethin', Jacob, and I want you to listen good. I wasn't always a Rebel. I was a quiet man, living on my land, and I didn't want no trouble." He stepped closer, lowering his voice. "Last summer the Yankees came down from Iowa and Illinois. They flopped their tents all over these hills till a man couldn't look one direction or another without seein' 'em. Well, I was glad they came, for I sided with the Union. I rested easy, knowin' they'd protect us all, and keep the peace." He gave a sad little chuckle. "Shoot, the Yankees helped themselves to three of our hogs one day without askin'. I let it go; figured they had to eat, same as me."

Even though Maggie'd told me about Clem being a Union man, the words hit me so strange, I gawked at him half a minute before I managed to ask, "What happened?"

"Asa Wheeler did me dirty. Aw, it's a long story—"

"Tell it!" I demanded. Clem owed me some explaining and I intended to stay put till I got it.

Clem motioned for me to follow him and began walking slowly up the drive. Calhoun trotted happily at his heels like he was going along on a hunt. "Along about two years ago Asa sold me a horse, sight unseen. He swore to me it was a fine horse, sayin' he was only sellin' because he needed the cash. I gave him fifty dollars, but when he delivered the horse I could see right off it was a broken-down, good-for-nothin' old thing. I told Asa I wanted my money back, but he wouldn't give it. Well, when I took it before the county judge, Asa swore I was the one who'd broke down the horse after I bought it."

"You torched Asa's house for that?"

"Just listen up. The judge sided with me; forced Asa to take his old horse back and return my money. Well, I guess you seen by now that Asa ain't one to forgive and forget. Ever since then, he had a score to settle."

"But what's that got to do with you turnin' Rebel?" I asked, confused.

"I'm gettin' to it!" Clem stopped walking and glanced toward the house as he lowered his voice. "One day last July Asa sent word he wanted to see me. Sounded like he wanted to make things right between us. Well, I figured it was high time, so I took Lazarus and set off for Asa's place. I'd gone near to halfway when five soldiers in blue came bustin' up out of the woods. They stuck their rifles in my face, yanked me down off my mule, and dragged me off to their camp with my hands tied."

My ears would hardly let Clem's words into my head. The Yankees were good folk. "They must have been foolin'...or drunk!" I thought out loud.

"No, Jacob. They had a warrant for my arrest. Asa'd gone and told them I was Secesh. Made up stories about how I'd been givin' food and shelter to bushwhackers and such; that I was plottin' against the Union. They waved a paper in my face that Asa'd signed, sayin' just that."

"But—"

"The soldiers were hard as this frozen ground," Clem cut me off. "They threw me in their camp jail and didn't give me but one drink of water the whole two days I was there." Clem pressed his lips together and swallowed hard like he was trying to choke down the memory. "They pushed my face in the dirt, callin' me Rebel scum. And when I tried to tell them I was a Union man just like them, they laughed in my face." Clem's lips began to tremble and he swiped at a runaway tear sliding down his nose. He breathed deep a minute and steadied his voice. "They said they'd take my farm away from me, and set my wife and baby runnin' if I didn't take the oath. Well, I was hungry, and scared, and nigh ready to drop from bein' tired. By then I hated the Yankees. I did what they wanted, but I cursed myself for doin' it. I took the oath so they'd leave Margaret alone. I couldn't stand to think of her bein' hurt."

"You never told her that!" I said, recalling what Maggie had said the day we passed by Asa's burnt-up house.

"No. I'd trusted the Union and the Union betrayed me. I didn't want to take away her trust too. But I knew I had to go on the warpath. Those Yankees made a Rebel out of me just as surely as they meant to make me the opposite."

I shut my eyes and shook my head as his words sank in. "And Asa?"

"He denied it all, like the low-down, night-crawlin' possum he is. Said it must have been a mistake! But I knew better. I was bitter mad, Jacob. Well, you know what I done next...."

I nodded.

"I ain't sayin' I did right," Clem went on. "I was hardly thinkin' straight when I went over there. I'm just sayin' why I did it. Never mind Asa. These hills are full of Federals wantin' to tell men like me what to do and what not to do. They're doin' it here in Missouri and in every other Southern state. Well, they ain't earned the right to force people into livin' their lives a certain way. They've stuck their nose in my business and slapped my family, my future, and my beliefs in the face. No Yankee nation's gonna rule over me, and I pity the poor fools who let 'em. Sure, I took the oath a second time, to protect Margaret. But Joel ought to know that when a man's forced to make a promise, that promise don't come from deep down inside him. No man's gonna live up to an oath he didn't take of his own free will!"

I didn't even try to hide my tears then. Clem looked at the sky till I got control again.

"Federals just saved your life!" I bawled.

"Still, I'll be beholdin' to no Yankee. There's bad folk on both sides, Jacob. But if I stay, my trouble ain't even started here. They won't rest till they've kilt me. And I won't rest till every last one of 'em is driven out of Missouri! They stole from me what I would've freely given, Jacob. My hogs...and my loyalty."

Clem reached into his coat pocket and pulled out a kerchief to wipe his nose. Just as quick he stuck it back in, but not before the red-stitched words on it jumped out at me: Our Father…Heaven…Hallered.

"Now you stay behind!" he ordered his dog, then turned to go. Shivering, I watched him tramp up the drive in his worn-down boots. When he'd nearly reached the road, something inside me spun me around and I raced toward the barn.

Sally tossed her head and snorted when she saw me coming at her. Standing close to her on winter mornings felt like wrapping myself up in a thick, warm blanket against the cold, and I'd always looked forward to seeing her when I'd dragged myself out of bed at chore time. She pressed her nose against my chest, looking for food. I lay my cold cheek on her warm one and circled my arms around her neck, feeling a lump rising in my throat. What did I need her for anyway?

Four months had gone by since I'd lost my folks, and I'd lately come to wonder if my home might not be here, with Maggie. Why, my kinfolk in Iowa were strangers compared to her! Even if I could find their farm, who's to say my family would be there? Who's to say my family was even alive? I'd been foolish, thinking I could ever meet up with them again; I'd let hope struggle on long enough. It was time to put it to rest.

Now Eliza was so thick with Maggie she'd even sewn Clem a hanky. Well, maybe I ought to be glad about that. Maybe I ought to make my peace with Missouri as best I could, and stay right where I was. Lazarus was healthy, and strong enough to do the work of two Sallys; we had all we needed here.

Not taking time to saddle the horse, I grabbed up a small feed sack and stuffed it full of oats from the feed barrel. I slung it over my shoulder and rushed to slip Sally's bridle over her head.

"Come on!" I coaxed as I yanked on the halter and led her outside. I stopped a minute and strained my eyes. Clem had turned west on the road; I could see him through the dogwood branches, taking big, long steps, his rifle shining in the gray morning light.

"Wait!" I called, pulling Sally after me as I chased him. He kept right on walking, so I called louder when I reached the road. He stopped. "Take Sally!" I panted as I drew closer, my chest aching from sucking in the cold air.

The bushwhacker's eyes widened.

"Go on, take her," I said. "How're you gonna get yourself down to Arkansas without a horse?"

"I reckoned I'd walk." We both looked down at his ragged boots, the ones I'd worn until Maggie'd bought me my own. Metzger never had made him that new pair. I grabbed hold of his hand and stuck Sally's lead into it, backing away so he couldn't hand it back. I tossed the feed sack to the ground near his feet.

Clem bent to pick up it up, then moved closer to Sally. He reached up and stroked her forelock. "She's a fine one, Jacob," he mumbled. "I'm proud to take her if you truly mean to give her to me."

I nodded. "You need her more than I do." I waited a second, staring at him. He'd changed. Or maybe I had. Standing there holding onto my horse was just a plain old Missouri farmer, ready to fight for what he believed in. "One more thing," I added. "The Yankees had no right to do what they did. I'm sorry they did it, Clem."

Clem looked down at the snowy ground and chawed on the inside of his cheeks a minute. "Well, I reckon you know I'm sorry too. Sorry for what all you been through." He stared down the road. "If we outlive this war, Jacob, let's see to it one like it don't happen again. Least not the way it's happened in Missouri."

I grabbed hold of his hand and stuck Sally's lead into it.

Suddenly I didn't want to see Clem touch my Sally. I gave her up of my own free will, but the minute they rode away together, my best chance of going north went with them. I squeezed my eyes shut tight while he swung himself onto her bare back and kicked her flanks with his worn-down boot heels. When I looked again they were already down the road a piece. I watched them top the next two hills until they turned south and disappeared, Sally's hoofbeats dying away with the last of the night.

Calhoun chased Clem part of the way, but when I called him back he came. He flopped his rear end down right next to my foot and sat whimpering. I stroked his neck.

Trudging back toward the house, I tried to blink away my tears. I thought how if our places had been reversed—if he'd been bushwhacked and I'd been threatened by Federals—I might be a Rebel and Clem a Union man. Well, I couldn't blame him, knowing how they'd done him wrong. I hoped he wouldn't blame me either, considering what his kind had done to me. Then I smiled a little, and the smile warmed my insides.

As I neared the house, I looked up and saw Maggie in her bedroom window. By the time I'd kicked the snow off my boots at the back doorstep, she'd come downstairs. Standing by the table, her eyes wet, she hugged herself inside a shawl thrown over her nightdress.

"He couldn't rest till he went south, Jacob," she said. "He couldn't change himself back into a Union man."

"Yes, ma'am."

"He'll be a real soldier now. It's better this way."

~

Maggie smiled at suppertime, talking about the war ending soon and what all needed to be done that spring around the farm. She talked about the way Jimmy was busting out of all his britches and wasn't it high time she got to work sewing him some new ones, and she figured Eliza'd be able to sew him some what with all the fine stitching she'd done lately. Me, I just stared down at my cornmeal mush, not wanting it.

Late that night when the fire burned low and Jimmy and Eliza slept, I went to my room and pulled the hickory bowl I'd carved for my ma out from beneath my bed. Wiping the dust from its newspaper wrapping, I carried it downstairs and set it in Maggie's lap.

"What's this?" she said, startled, for she'd been staring blank-eyed into the fire. She unwrapped it slow and careful, turning it around and around in the light of the dying flames. "You did fine work, Jacob. I'm proud to own it." She rose out of her chair and pulled a stool over to the high corner cupboard. "I'll put it up where pretty things should be."

My chest feeling full, I looked down, scraping my bare toe back and forth on the plank floor. "Well, I'll go on up to bed now," I mumbled.

Maggie turned and looked down at me from the stool. "I'm grateful to have a man on the farm, Jacob. We'll get by."

Climbing the stairs, I felt myself wandering somewhere between hurt and satisfaction. I'd fought for Clem only to see him up and leave us. Still, I guessed he had a right to go and do his fighting in a proper way. He'd chosen the truest road for himself, and I'd chosen the best road for Eliza and me. Maggie needed a man on her farm. Clem might be gone, but Maggie could count on me.

Snow fell on and off all that week. Spring had come and gone like the bushwhacker himself, full of promises, but hard put to live up to them. We went through each cold, gray day, not saying much, just keeping up with our chores and amusing ourselves as best we could before the fire each night.

I hauled more firewood up from the creek woods. When I passed Clem's fire pit I spied something I'd missed before—the rabbit skin still hanging stretched between the two stick poles, dried stiff and frozen in the icy wind. Realizing I'd dropped and never picked up the one Clem gave me, I looked around for it. It was gone; a fox or some such animal had carried it off. I untied the one between the poles and threw it in the wagon with the wood, thinking if I could soften it up, Maggie'd finally get that pair of gloves Clem wanted her to have.

Susannah came up of an evening, bringing along a basket of wool to pick burrs out of by the fire, or a quilt to piece with Eliza. My sister picked out the burrs peaceably enough, but those two fussed and hollered over that quilt a good deal. Eliza wanted to sew one big star in the center of the quilt, but the old woman would have none of it.

"No quilt can bear a single star without bringing bad luck on the entire household!" she declared, and she showed Eliza how to arrange the pieces into a whole mess of stars across the blanket. She called it "Carpenter's Wheel," and the two of them sat hunched over by the oil lamp, pushing their needles up and down, in and out.

Henry tagged along with his wife, but he never played his fiddle anymore. He mostly sat quiet next to the fire, resting his chin in his hands. When Susannah wasn't sewing or picking burrs out of her wool, she took turns with Maggie, rocking and singing to Jimmy. Otherwise, Jimmy'd crawl around the room or pull himself up and hang on to the furniture, leaving a trail of slobber everywhere he went.

By and by we got word of the big battle down at Pea Ridge, Arkansas, just across the state line. General Price had tried his best to march his Rebel men into Missouri again, but the Yankees met him on the snowy hills and beat him back. The Yankees even killed General McCulloch. Henry figured after a whipping like that the Rebels would head south and stay there, but I wasn't so sure.

Sometimes Henry brought a newspaper up to the house and asked me to read the war news to him. Not long after we heard about Pea Ridge, I read about the two monster ships that fought on the sea back east. Henry's mouth dropped open when I told him how the Merrimack and the Monitor fought for four hours and hardly even scratched each other because they were both covered with iron. I myself was hard pressed to imagine any of it, for I'd never seen a ship, let alone a sea. How could iron ships float? How could they fight so long without sinking?

I asked if Henry'd ever been acquainted with such things.

He shook his head no. "Iron-covered fighting ships!" he exclaimed. "Only the good Lord can imagine what else folk will come up with in the way of war weapons."

I felt afraid when he said that, wondering what could come next.

But Henry was more bothered by the news he'd been hearing about the Union army back in Virginia. It seemed they were just sitting around, stuck to their spot, while that sly Rebel General Jackson ran circles around them. It appeared the Union General, McClellan, wouldn't budge.

"What that fool needs is a good swift kick in the hindquarters!" raged Henry one night at Maggie's supper table. "I'd lend my boot to do the job iffen I could just get close enough to him! I'd kindle a fire under that man's behind iffen only they'd let me!"

"Ye just stay home and kindle my cook fire, Henry Wilkinson, or I'll lend my boot to yer behind!" threatened Susannah. That hushed him up, at least long enough for him to finish his beans and hoecake.

～

Spring finally broke through and held its ground. The black sow had six shoats and the barn swallows started in building their nests out of the mud left by the melting snow. Iowa still came to mind from time to time, but I pushed it aside. Even Eliza had left off asking me about going north. Maggie's place was as much home as anywhere. Her fields needed attention, and it was high time to think about planting.

One morning after I'd plowed two furrows, I looked across the field to see Eliza coming my way. She stumbled along with a heavy sack of seed wheat slung over her shoulder.

"I'll plow now. You plant awhile," she puffed and panted as she drew up close, dropping the sack to the ground. "Then we'll switch."

"You're goin' to plow? Stop foolin'!" I laughed.

"I said I'll plow and you plant," she insisted, tucking some loose yellow hair back beneath her bonnet.

"But plowin's men's work!"

Eliza's face went blood red and she barreled up close and gave me a shove. "Now listen here, Jacob Knight. Clem ain't here to do his share of the work, and you ain't but half his size. I figure it's goin' to take you and me both workin' our hardest to get the plantin' done in time. We don't want to be stuck with no harvest come fall!"

She had a point, but I still couldn't picture her behind a plow. "Does Maggie know you're out here?"

Eliza sighed and rolled her eyes. "You think I wouldn't tell her where I was off to?" Then, tired of waiting for my say-so, she grabbed hold of the plow handles and clucked to Lazarus, forgetting to slip the plow strap around her. The mule took off with her barely keeping up, the heavy plow reeling from side to side and her skinny arms trying their best to guide it straight. I laughed out loud, but she turned around and shot me a spitting mad look, so I shut up. I picked up the sack of seed wheat and got down to the business of planting.

⁓

One afternoon about a month after Clem left, when the red-bud trees were just beginning to bloom, Henry came hobbling up the drive, fast as he could. Catching sight of Maggie beating a rug in the yard, he called out to her, waving both arms high in the air. I stopped plowing to watch him come. Something white was in his hand. Leaving the mule and plow in the middle of the field, I ran for the house, getting there just as Henry did. The old man's shouts had brought Eliza out on the porch too, wiping floury hands on her apron.

"A letter, Maggie!" Henry panted. "Postman brought it out from Linneus today. Said it's from Arkansas."

"Thank you, Pa." Maggie took it from his hand and opened it slowly. She held up a white paper with fancy handwriting. Her eyes scurried back and forth across the page as she sank down onto a porch step, her lips silently mouthing the words she read.

We waited. Jimmy toddled out the front door and across the porch in bare legs and feet, grinning big and showing all eight of his teeth. He dropped to all fours and scooted himself over to the porch rail, where he pulled himself upright and clawed in the air toward Maggie.

"Ma! Ma!" he squealed.

Startled, she looked up at him, then from Jimmy to Henry, me, and then Eliza. She made like she wanted to speak, but no words came out, so she handed me the letter and held out her arms to her son. When she'd pulled him onto her lap, wrapping her arms around him tight, she lay her head on his and squeezed her eyes shut.

"Read it to me, boy," said Henry. "Ye know I never did have the benefit of schoolin'."

My hand shook till the paper rattled, but I cleared my throat and made out the fancy script as best I could.

Dear Mrs. Canaday,

It becomes my painful duty to inform you of the death of Clement Canaday, a member of my company. He departed this life the 7th of March, respected by all his comrades. His remains were laid beside his brothers in arms who have fallen with him. His friends have my heartfelt sympathies in this their bereavement. May it comfort you that he fell fighting for the glorious cause of Southern freedom.

I enclose for you a cutting of his hair. Accept my good wishes...

I looked up at Maggie. "It's signed by the Captain of the 8th Missouri under General Price. 'Neath that it says 'Fayetteville, Arkansas.'"

"Well I'll be hanged," whispered Henry. "Clem fought at Pea Ridge."

Maggie held out her hand and I placed the letter in it. She tipped the envelope and a strand of brown hair fell out into her palm. White-faced and dry-eyed, she looked at us all.

"You all got to understand one thing," she said. "This ain't no tragedy. This is what Clem wanted. I'm proud he died a soldier, and not a bushwhacker. You all can be proud too." Then she set Jimmy down beside her on the step and got to her feet. As she stepped down into the yard, a gusty wind came up, wrapping her skirt around her legs and pulling loose some hair from the knot at the back of her head. Suddenly, with all her might, she flung Clem's hairs up into the air. The wind whipped them up high, scattering them across the yard and over the cornfield.

Just after sunup next day, Susannah walked up to the house dressed in a black bonnet with a long linen veil hanging down behind her. She climbed up on a chair and pulled the hickory bowl I'd carved down off the corner cupboard. Carrying it out to the garden, she scooped up a handful of earth to lay in one half of it. Then back inside she went, straight to the kitchen. She pinched up some salt from the saltbox, sprinkling it over the plate's other half. We all watched her set the dish on the mantel and bow her head in silence.

"What is it?" I whispered, drawing up alongside her.

"Earth for the flesh," she replied. "Salt for the spirit. May Clem's spirit return to the good Lord who made it."

At dinner Maggie said we might as well make sure the whole county knew Clem died honorably on the battlefield, and would I mind going in to Linneus to place a notice in the Bulletin? So next morning I headed off to town on Lazarus.

Leave-taking

The refugee camp at Linneus had swelled up so big by then that homeless families were spilling over into the streets. I tethered Lazarus in front of the millinery and went about my errands. On my way back to the mule, I passed along the edge of the camp, for I had no desire to walk through it anymore. There was no use listening for a voice I knew, or looking for a familiar face. Just being among folk who shared our troubles brought back all I was trying to forget.

At the camp's edge, an old man with only one tooth on top sat sunning himself on an overturned cookpot. His head hung down and he scratched the back of his neck where vermin had probably bit. When he saw me passing by he straightened up and called out, "Natchez fell —Yankees just heard it by telegraph! 'Fore that, Baton Rouge! 'Fore that, New Orleans! Pretty soon the whole cotton-pickin' South'll fall!"

"That's good news," I replied, nodding my thanks and pushing on past him. There was no time for lingering. The women in camp were busy making ready with the noonday meal, and I was hungry. Smelling their food made me eager to hurry home for Maggie's fine cooking.

The May sun made even the dingy gray tents shine white. Barefoot children climbed up on wagon tongues and stuck their fingers in their mouths, gawking at me. A woman sat suckling her child beneath a lean-to, streaks of sunshine falling across her through its wide cracks. She stared right past me like I wasn't there. I dropped my eyes to the ground, hoping she'd be feeding her baby in a proper home soon.

My heart weighed heavy as I walked back to Lazarus. I slowed my steps. Looking up at the clear blue sky, I thanked God my lot hadn't been the same as the pitiful folks around me. Before I could say "Amen," I tripped and nearly stumbled. Something lay at my feet.

"Baby, get on back here," called a woman's voice. "You don't belong in folks' way."

I'd run headlong into a small child, taking its first toddling steps on bare, dusty feet. She wore a faded, too-small calico dress with the seams let out below the arms. I bent down and turned her toward her ma's voice, and as I looked down into her tiny face she smiled, showing me four pretty new teeth.

"Jerusha, you come on, now."

My gut spun like a wheel on an upended wagon. I knew that voice. I straightened up and looked around me for the woman who'd called my sister's name. She stood behind a rising cloud of steam, stirring something in a kettle over an open fire. I picked up the child and moved closer to the woman.

"Did you call this child Jerusha?" I asked, coming up alongside her. She wiped her forehead with a corner of her skirt, then turned toward me.

It was Ma.

"Jacob!" she cried, letting the spoon clank into the pot. Her hands flew to her mouth and she gaped at me, wide-eyed. Then she reached out her arms to me, and I rushed to feel them around me again. She hugged Jerusha and me tight and cried hot tears onto my hair, then held me at arm's length.

"Eliza?" she whispered.

"She's all right, Ma!"

"Oh, thank the Lord!" She broke down sobbing then, hanging on to me for dear life. I clung to her just as tight till she got control of herself, wiping her face with her dress sleeve. "We thought we'd lost you for good!" she whispered, taking one long, satisfied look at my face. Her own face was thinner now, tanned and toughened by hard times, but her soft, familiar voice hadn't changed one bit. "Ma, where's Pa? And Sarah?"

Ma looked startled. She wheeled around and cried, "Ezra!" A tent flap behind her opened up. Out stepped my pa and sister Sarah, wearing a patched-up dress so big it was hanging off one shoulder. She was still a tiny thing, though she'd grown half a head in seven months' time.

My pa reached out his left hand to me and I noticed then that the right one dangled limp at his side.

He saw me staring. "They got me, son, right in the arm."

"That night?" I asked. I could almost hear Pa crying out in pain as Eliza and I ran from the house.

"Yes, the Rebels. It ain't been the same since. But I get by."

I threw my arms around his neck and hugged him hard. The dirty bushwhackers had crippled Pa and kept us apart all these months! I hated them as much as I ever had, and a murdering fury flashed through me like lightning. But another thought thundered close behind: the sight of Clem lying trussed up beneath the walnut tree with a noose around his neck. I recalled Joel's words, and admitted to myself once more that he was right. Missouri's bloodletting had gone too far, lasted too long. Vengeance didn't belong to me; it never had. Like Joel Wilkinson, Jacob Knight would do his best to stop up the wounds.

"You didn't come back for us," I croaked, a big, choking sob catching me in the throat.

Ma pulled me down beside her onto an overturned wash bucket. She wrapped her arms around me and held me close. "Your pa near to died that night," she explained, trembling. "He was hit in the chest and shoulder, and was bleeding bad. When the bushwhackers rode off, I dragged him out of the burning house. Oh, Jacob, it was all I could do to load him into the handcart, what with the little one crying and Sarah tugging at my skirts."

So she, and not the bushwhackers, had dumped the corn and made off with the handcart.

"He was bleeding so badly, son. I wheeled him and the girls along the Fayette road in the dark, on and on until I was like to drop. Thank God a farmer from Franklin came riding toward us on his way to Boonesboro. He turned around and led us to a doctor back near his home...then took us in. I wasn't myself, Jacob. By the time I thought to send someone back to look for you it was past noon the next day."

"Soon as my wounds healed up," continued Pa, "we started out looking for you. We've been everywhere between here and Jefferson City, asking about you. I've been riding out just about every day, knocking on doors, talking to folks. I aimed to do it hereabouts, starting today. We only just arrived last night."

Ma broke down and sobbed. "Oh, thank God, Ezra! Now we can all go on up to Iowa together."

"Eliza and me, we thought maybe you'd gone up there without us," I confessed. "We ought to have known you wouldn't do it! I wondered all this time what'd happened to you. I'd almost given up hope...."

Ma hugged me to her again. Our handcart stood behind the tent my folks had been given by the Federals. Tethered to it was the sorriest old buckskin mare I'd ever seen.

Pa saw me looking at her. "A gift from the Yankees," he chuckled. "They couldn't use her anymore." I opened my mouth to tell them we'd found Sally in the brush and rode her north, but I shut it again quick before I spoke. What I'd done with Sally, they might not understand. Still, I had no regrets.

We'd lost near to everything that night, I thought, but at least now we had each other.

Sarah peeked out at me from behind Ma's skirt, sticking her finger in her mouth, but Jerusha ran right to me, stretching out her arms. I laughed outright to see her walking on her own two feet like a big girl, for she hadn't been but a crawling baby last October. I grabbed her up and gave her a kiss on the cheek, holding her there till she squealed and squirmed to get down again.

"Where were you this long while, Jacob?" asked Pa. "How'd you get by?"

"You come with me," I said. "I'll show you."

∼

Maggie walked out onto her porch as we clopped and creaked up the drive with the buckskin mare and the handcart. Calhoun trotted out from behind the house and climbed the porch steps, sitting down beside her. Maggie watched as we drew closer, me walking beside my ma and holding on to her hand. All at once she seemed to figure out how things stood with us. Without turning around, she called for Eliza to come.

I let go of Ma and ran ahead to Maggie. She was leaning back on the pillar post like she needed help standing. Behind her Eliza burst out the front door and flew down the steps, squealing with joy. I grabbed hold of Maggie's arm and said, "Maggie? They're here. Ma and Pa came to fetch us."

She turned slowly to look in my face, and though she was no more than half a foot away from me her eyes seemed to gaze out from a deep, dark place. "That's fine, Jacob," she softly said, stroking my hair and looking back toward my oncoming family. Pulling herself away from me, she walked down the steps and right up to Ma with an outstretched hand, but not before I saw her wipe away a tear.

After Maggie sent me to her folks' cabin to bring back an armload of wool coverlets, my family spread them on the floor of the attic room that had been home to Eliza and me. There we slept, crowded but happy. It was the first real roof my folks had had over their heads since last October.

Maggie kept us all for another month. With his one good arm, Pa tried his best to help me finish Clem's share of the spring farm work. Together we broke up the fallow ground and planted corn and wheat where Clem had told me he wanted it.

Ma and Eliza helped Maggie turn the earth in her garden, then planted carrots, beets, turnips, and squash.

"Your girl's been a mighty hand at keepin' house lately, Myra," Maggie told Ma. "I've been proud to have her to help."

Eliza blushed red and crouched down to pull up an earthworm for the chickens. She tossed it in a bucket, looking across the yard at me like she hoped I wouldn't tell Ma that things had ever been any different. I shook my head and moved off toward the barn. As I went I heard Ma reply, "Well, now there's welcome news. I always knew she'd decide to lend a helping hand one day, all on her own."

I held down a laugh as I walked away. Looking back, I saw that Maggie was doing the same. In the evenings after supper Maggie, Ma, and Eliza sat on the front porch in the late-setting sun and sewed Jimmy new clothes cut out of Clem's old ones. Susannah stitched right along with them, for she and Henry came up to see us just about every evening.

Henry growled like a bear and hobbled around chasing Jimmy, Jerusha, and Sarah, making Sarah squeal and race toward the walnut tree with the little ones toddling behind her. Just when he'd settle himself down to rest they'd come sneaking back to the front steps, giggling and begging him to do it again. As they ran all over the place raising a ruckus I thought that for now, at least, Maggie had what she said she'd always wanted: a house full of laughing children.

One evening Pa and I were feeding the livestock when Henry turned up at the barn door. His hounds yelped and ran circles around him like always, but Henry made like he didn't even see them. He eased himself down onto a bale of straw. The dogs settled at his feet, their pink, slobbery tongues hanging to the ground.

"Got war news in town today," he said, staring at nothing. By the look of him I figured it was bad news for the Union.

"Speak out, Henry," urged Pa. "More fighting in Missouri?"

Henry shook his head and ran both hands through his stubbly white hair like he always did when something wasn't quite right inside of him.

"Go on, Henry," I said, squatting at his feet and stroking a hound's head. I looked up into his face. "Tell us what. Union got beat somewhere?"

"Naw," he answered in a voice we could barely hear. "Naw, I guess it was a Union victory all right. Place called Shiloh Church, back in Tennessee."

"Why then, that's good news!" I cried, slapping a hand on his knee and shaking it. "Ain't you happy about it, Henry?" Pa and I smiled at each other.

"I was till I heard the particulars." Henry rested his elbows on his knees and cradled his forehead in his hands. "Each side lost a heap of men, nigh two thousand each. And sixteen thousand hurt. I didn't know so many men could get kilt all at one time!"

"Lord have mercy!" gasped Pa. "Such a many!"

"Folk are sayin' more died there than ever before in this war," Henry went on. "Boys, I reckon hate'll run high after a slaughter like that. This fight's like to go on and on. I'd hoped the Federals would horsewhip and hog-tie the South good and quick, and bring 'em to their senses. But I fear it ain't to be."

Pa and I didn't eat much supper that night. How could so many men die in two days' fight? We'd never before heard the like. And if the war dragged on, what would become of Missouri? Would her own people tear her to shreds while they clawed and kicked and fought over her?

After that night I still prayed the Union to win, but I never whooped and hollered again at war news. I just wished the whole sorry mess would be done with so Missouri's folk could stick their broken lives back together.

But news about the Yankees capturing a Confederate island down the Mississippi River brought out Henry's old fighting spirit again, till he even forgot his misery over Shiloh Church. In fact, he put on such a hollering war dance in Maggie's front yard, she sent my Pa out to drag him inside, for fear he'd spook the livestock.

"Hallelujah! Hallelujah! First New Orleans and now this! We're hittin' 'em from both sides!" rejoiced Henry at the top of his lungs. "I knew it! Didn't I tell ye the Yankees would make short work of it—didn't I tell ye?"

"You told us aplenty," laughed Pa, laying his good arm across Henry's shoulders and leading him inside the house. "Last week you told us the war was going to drag on, now you say it'll end quick—which is it, Captain Henry?"

"Well, Ezra, ye fetch me a mug of cider and I'll tell ye," chuckled the old warrior, and he slapped my pa on the back.

⌒

When June turned to July, and we finished the hay-making, Pa decided it was time for us to move north. We'd stayed to help Maggie as long as we could before losing fair-weathered travel time. Maggie baked up extra corncakes and packed them for our journey, along with whatever else she could spare from down cellar. Pa tried to tell her not to, but she just said that feeding a woman and a baby didn't take much and she had way more than she could use anyway. I knew better, but giving was her way.

The Yankees were sitting pretty by then in the northern counties, though we still heard tell of bushwhacking going on here and there. But Pa'd decided it made no sense to stay any longer where we had no home and no kinfolk. We'd get on up to Iowa just as quick as we could and be done with this whole sorry mess called Missouri.

The morning we said good-bye day dawned without a cloud. I rose at sunup and packed my few belongings in an old haversack. After I dressed I folded Clem's nightshirt and laid it on my pillow, running my fingers gently across it for the last time. I wished I could give Clem back to Maggie, and not just his old nightshirt.

Before going downstairs I crossed to the window and looked out once more over Maggie's land. She had two fields of wheat near ready for harvest, and a half-grown corn crop, besides. "How'll she do it all?" I fretted. "It's more than a woman alone can handle!" But I knew Henry and Susannah would lend a hand with the reaping and the shucking.

After Maggie fed us breakfast, she and Jimmy walked us to where our cart stood, loaded and newly greased at the axles. Ma hugged and thanked her, and so did Pa. Eliza locked her arms around Maggie and buried her face in her apron, just about having to be peeled off of her.

"I always said to Jacob that you been as good a ma as our own! Didn't I say it, Jacob?"

"Yes, Eliza, you did," I said.

Tears ran down Maggie's cheeks and dripped off onto her dress but her mouth was set in that same hard, straight line she'd worn the first night my sister and I came to her farm.

Calhoun pressed his nose against my knee. I took his muzzle in both my hands and touched my nose to his soft, cold one. "You got a big job to do now," I told him. "Missouri's needin' all the good watchdogs it can get nowadays."

I cinched Old Silas's saddle around the Yankee horse's belly and helped Eliza up. We'd be lucky if this used-up nag even got us to the border. Thinking how I'd handed our finest mare to a Rebel, I half laughed and half cried inside. Maybe I'd been a fool. Yet somehow giving Sally to Clem had made me feel like I'd wrapped a clean cotton cloth around at least one of

Missouri's festering wounds, the way Maggie had cleaned and wrapped my cut feet when I first came to her.

Sarah and Jerusha sat in the handcart, cuddling a young pig, for Maggie'd handed my ma the biggest and best of her sow's litter as a parting gift. I led the horse on account of my pa not having the strength to hold her if she bolted, and my folks walked beside the cart.

Maggie followed us up the drive, leaning against the rail fence to watch us go. She set Jimmy down to balance on his own two feet a minute before he tottered and clung on to her skirt for dear life. How tiny he'd been when Eliza and I came here last October! Suddenly I realized that I hadn't said a proper good-bye to the boy. I handed Pa the horse's lead and walked back. Kneeling down beside Jimmy, I ran my fingers through the shock of red hair he'd sprouted like a patch of winter wheat.

"Good-bye Jimmy. Take care of your mama," I murmured.

Maggie hoisted him up onto her hip. "We'll get by, Jacob. Now you'd best join your folks."

"Yes ma'am." I turned once more to watch her standing in the morning sun, waving good-bye. She looked so small against the cornfield and the sky; so frail beneath the weight of the life I left her to. But she was strong deep down, where it counted. Walking away, I knew that strength would get her by.

Leading the horse in Pa's place, it occurred to me that manhood lay just ahead on the road, coming at me quick, like a tomahawk spinning through the air. The child that Maggie had taken in last fall still wandered around back there somewhere in her cornfields, calling out to me, begging me to turn around again and again. I knew I'd never forget the sight of her standing there in her butternut homespun. She'd been both ma and pa to me for half a year. As I walked away I thought how for me and Eliza, this was the second such good-bye.

My own ma seemed to know I hurt inside. She quickened her steps and came up beside me, laying her arm across my shoulders.

Before long we drew up near Henry's cabin. The old man stood on the porch beside Susannah, waiting for us to drive by. He held himself straight and tall, his rifle slung over one shoulder, his pack of dogs lying at his feet. I could tell he meant to watch us go without speaking. Susannah puffed on her pipe, her hands on her hips, her proud face set like a stone. As we passed, Henry nodded his head once. I pulled the tomahawk out of my belt and waved it above my head to show him I'd never forget him.

Epilogue

Fall 1931

Now I've reached the age of eighty-three. This summer, my daughter asked me was there anywhere special I wanted to go. I said yes, I'd like to go down to Missouri one more time. She had no objection, for it isn't but three hours' drive from my home in Iowa. Well, I never thought I'd see the day when folks could travel so fast from one place to another. She packed us up a picnic lunch and we made the trip in her car.

The hills hadn't changed much. Corn covered more of them than it used to, but now there were a whole lot more people around. Where the corn didn't grow, prairie grass still grew tall and thick, with wildflowers scattered across it like stitches on a quilt.

Though I'd been away sixty-nine years, I hadn't forgotten the way to Maggie's place, and we found it easily. My heart flopped in my chest as we motored up the drive. It took only a second for me to realize the place stood empty. The old house had surrendered to the years, the ragged remains of a curtain flapping in the warm breeze. The front door swung to and fro in the wind, banging shut again and again; the barn creaked and sagged beneath the weight of time gone by. Grass marched across the fields that Clem had plowed, fluttering like the pages of a book. The book he'd written in the earth.

"Let's go," I said. I couldn't bear to look anymore. Oh, I don't know what I'd expected. I knew Maggie'd be gone, of course, but I guess I'd hoped her son Jimmy would be there, or his children.

We drove on up to the churchyard and spread out our picnic. The old church had fared better than Maggie's farm; someone had painted it not long ago, and the glass in the windows remained, unbroken. After we'd eaten, I wandered amongst the tombstones, and there I found them all, the ones I'd come to see. They lay asleep beneath my feet, beneath the stones that told me their stories.

Maggie had married again. She'd lived to see many a grandchild. It comforted me to know she hadn't lived out her life alone. Henry and Susannah lay side by side, having lived long too. I took out my pocketknife and cut away the grass that'd grown up around their stones, then ran my fingers along the letters of their names. I felt sorry I hadn't come down to see them while they still walked on this side of the earth, but long years of raising crops and a family had tied me down.

Turning in a circle till I felt sure I faced south, toward Arkansas, I whispered my good-byes to Clem. I still wasn't sure how I felt about that bushwhacker, but I'd wandered into the enemy's camp and walked by his side long enough to see the war through his eyes. He was just a man, after all—a man who had his own ideas and stuck to them, same as I'd stuck to mine. I'd never stopped being a Union man, but the sharp blade of hatred had been dulled forever in me by knowing Clem Canaday, and by almost seeing him hang.

Then I did something an old man almost never does. I lay myself down in the warm, sweet grass with my hands behind my head, and watched the clouds crawl across the summer sky. Closing my eyes, I felt the earth hold me in warm, gentle hands, heard the leaves above me softly whispering. Cradled in Missouri's arms, I felt her comfort me. It was good to be home again.

When my daughter shook me awake and said it was time to go, it occurred to me that there was still one stone I hadn't seen. I paced up and down the rows until I found it. Half hidden behind the high, tough grass, moss had grown up in its carved letters. I yanked up the grass and scraped away the moss with my thumbnail.

Sheriff Joel Wilkinson had departed this life not long after I'd left Missouri, how I couldn't tell. But near the bottom of his stone was carved an epitaph. As I read it, I caught my breath and remembered the old circuit rider who'd whispered those words in this very place:

> *Blessed are the peacemakers,*
> *for they shall be called the children of God.*

Matthew 5:9

About the Author

Born in Seattle, Washington, Jennifer Johnson Garrity currently calls Germany home. She speaks German and French, and has lived in Europe with her family on and off for more than fifteen years. She and her husband have three children, each of whom was born in a different country.

Her interest in Missouri's difficult position during the Civil War began when she conducted extensive research into her grandmother's history.

This is Jennifer's first published work.

About the Illustrator

Paul Bachem has worked for many years as an award-winning freelance illustrator, producing work for most of the major book and magazine publishers in New York, across the country, and as far away as Sydney, Australia.

Some of his work is in the permanent collection of the Forbes Gallery in New York City.